Bob Allan

Border lays and other poems

Bob Allan

Border lays and other poems

ISBN/EAN: 9783744723152

Printed in Europe, USA, Canada, Australia, Japan

Cover: Foto ©Andreas Hilbeck / pixelio.de

More available books at **www.hansebooks.com**

BORDER LAYS

And other Poems

BY

ROBERT ALLAN

J. & R. PARLANE

PAISLEY

1891

Dedicatory Preface.

To you, my friends in my native town of Jedburgh and in our fair Borderland, I send this volume. I have entitled it, " Border Lays and other Poems," because it was written for most part by the Jed, the Teviot, and the Ale, and because at least the first division of the work contains references to Border scenes and places. My lot is now cast in another part of Scotland; but with affection I revert to you, O friends, and to the lovely banks and scaurs of Jed, and to the classic Teviot, and to the exquisitely beautiful *Aln* or Ale, in whose *crum* or crook lies that loveliest of villages, *Aln*crum or Ancrum.

Some of the poems in this volume are doubtless known to you, and that many of them are humble enough I am well aware; yet it is my hope that there is at least something here and there throughout the book that may tend to improve and ennoble. To inspire the soul with love for Nature and Nature's God; to inculcate a true and candid manhood; to rouse some nobler conception of our solidarity and bounden duty to be loving co-workers for those spiritual and moral renovations which we so deeply need—this in not a few of my poems has been my heart-felt purpose.

In connection with the Scottish poems in the volume allow me a word. Just as the heather and bluebells are

indigenous to our Scottish hills and moorlands, so our
Scottish poetry or pastoral and ballad song is indigenous
to the simple, perfervid Scottish mind and heart. The
mother-tongue expresses with wondrous grace and readiness
the feelings of the Scottish heart, and that its spell may be
irresistibly powerful many an "Old Scottish Emigrant"
can attest.   Trusting this volume may be favourably
received, I am, dear friends, yours faithfully,

ROBERT ALLAN.

REDHOUSE, GASSTOWN,
    DUMFRIES, *1st May, 1891.*

CONTENTS.

PART I.

Poems connected with the Scottish Border.

PART II.

Nature=Sketches and other Poems.

PART III.

Poems on Life and Duty.

PART IV.

Elegiac Poems.

BORDER LAYS.

THE OLD SCOTTISH EMIGRANT.

OH, my heart's in the Lowlands of Scotland ;
   Though my head is grown grey I still dream
Of the hame o' my faither and mither
   On the banks of the Teviot's bright stream.
The last time that e'er I beheld it,
   Round its porch bloom'd the jessamine fair ;
And the rooms were a' cosie and bonnie,
   For my faither and mither were there.

The garden, too, told o' their presence,
   Wi' its mint, thyme, and southernwood sweet ;
And here was the auld dial staunin',
   And there was the summer-house neat :
The summer-house where on fine Sabbaths,
   When the sun had begun to decline,
They would sit and would read frae the Bible,
   Or some worthy and learned divine.

The last time I stood in the garden,
  The young apples hung on the trees;
And among the sweetwilliams and roses
  Were humming battalions o' bees.
Frae the stackyard, too, came a blythe cacklin',
  As if hens there were laying away;
And the crummies for milkin' were mooin',
  For 'twas e'en the mid-time o' the day.

Yes, I felt a' was bonnie and cheerie—
  But, oh! I'd a weight on my heart,
For the moment was quickly approaching
  When frae a' I was gaen to depart.
As I stood there I kent that the auld folk
  In their chamber were prayin' for me—
Their son, their ae son sae beloved,
  Wha his fortune must seek owre the sea.

'Twas a moment unspeakably solemn,
  And I trow I right glad would hae been
To hae stoppit at hame wi' the auld folk
  Till Death's fingers had steekit their een.
I had lik'd gin I needna hae left them,
  But the chances were feeble and few
For a young man at hame, and they'd biddin'
  Me try what abroad I could do.

They had biddin' me gang, for to keep me
  They trow'd it would hardly be fair;
Yet I felt it was hard, hard to leave them,
  For o' trouble they'd had their fu' share.

Oh, I'd mony a thought 'bout my parents—
  Would I meet them again in their hame,
Or would I next meet them in heaven,
  Where ilk ane his ain folk may claim?

But I thought, too, concerning a sister
  Who wi' me by the 'Teviot had play'd,
Who had faded in life's early morning,
  Who in Ancrum kirkyaird we had laid.
Ah, I felt while that lov'd one's dear image
  Arose up so bright in my mind,
Just as if she were still 'mong the living,
  Whom now I was leaving behind.

Oh, the days when I went with that sister
  On the banks of the Teviot to rove,
Unto me looking back they seem'd shining
  Like links in some rare chain of love.
And when long, weary weakness had taken
  'That lov'd one so bright and so fair,
How oft would my mother entrust her
  To the faithful and strong brother's care.

And out in the sun I would carry
  The darling, and sit in some nook,
And amuse her for hours turning over
  The pages o' braw picture book.
And oft wi' gay flowers I would deck her,
  Until her fine beauty would seem
Not sae much like a mortal appearance
  As a something o' whilk ane might dream.

Yes, I grudg'd to forego the sweet pathways
　　She had made doubly sacred to me,
And the calm Sabbath times, ere the preaching,
　　When a while at her grave I could be.
Ah ! those scenes so belov'd and so hallow'd—
　　Those scenes, when again would I tread—
When again see that mound arching over
　　The dust of the dear, sacred dead ?

So I thought ; then the thought o' the auld folk
　　Rose boonmaist again in my mind ;
After a', it was mainly the living
　　I'd to grieve about leaving behind.
That on earth I might ne'er again see them,
　　I confess that I now had my fears ;
And yet looking around I saw many
　　Wha nummer'd a hantle mae years.

Oh, what though I ca'd them the auld folk,
　　My parents were rash yet and bauld,
And might see o' gude years still a decade,
　　Nor e'en be, after a', donnert auld.
Yes ; wha, wha could tell but kind Heaven
　　Might my heart's dearest wishes allow—
Wha could tell but I'd yet help my parents
　　When their coffers were toomer than now ?

And I e'en, staunin' there in the garden,
　　To plan and to study began—
Yes, yes, ance out here I would set me
　　To toil and to do like a man.

And when I had got a nice posey,
   I'd come hame and I'd buy a bit house;
And I'd tak' to mysel' the auld couple,
   And we'd a' live fu' cosie and crouse.

Yes, this was my plan, and wi' ardour
   My hale heart thereunto now inclin'd;
For though young, weel I kent I would never
   Belang to the marrying kind.
Though young, I had known in deep earnest
   What it is a fond lover to be;
But had found at the last, to my sorrow,
   That my fair was not destin'd for me.

It had been the auld story :—Twa worthies
   To the same goal and object had press'd;
But the ane had a chariot and horses,
   And by these o' the prize got possess'd.
Yet with joy I took Heaven now to witness
   That 'twas on my ain feet that I ran;
And that now, at the last, my sharp trial
   Had made me but more of a man.

So it was in the auld-fashion'd garden,
   In the far-away, bright summer prime,
That I spent—eh, whow me! weel I mind it—
   Some precious wee fraction o' time.
Then into the house I gaed quickly,
   And sat doon wi' a sair, burstin' heart
In my place, and commun'd wi' the auld folk,
   Till the clock chappin' bade me depart.

Yes, the clock chappin' bade me be ganging,
    And it sounded to me like a knell;
Yet I buckled mysel' for the pairting,
    Which was harder than ever I'll tell.
Ah, I buckled mysel' for the pairting,
    Though I saw from my parents right plain
That in spite o' my plans they were thinking
    That on earth we would ne'er meet again.

O hame, lovely hame by the Teviot!
    Well I mind the auld dog at the door,
How it yammer'd wi' grief while the auld folk
    Said—" Adieu, lad, we'll meet here no more.
Adieu! Since wi' us there is little,
    You maun e'en push your fortunes abroad;
But mind, lad, your faither and mither—
    Yes, mind them aye next to your God!

"Still mind what we've taught ye and made ye,
    Still mind what we wish you to be;
Rest sure that we're still praying for ye
    When you're far, far away o'er the sea.
Be faithful, be upright, be manly—
    A man baith in action and word;
Ah, mind we maun a' meet in heaven
    Through the merits and death o' the Lord."

Wi' tears and kind farewells we parted,
    And I ne'er saw the auld folk again;
They dee'd—there was short time between them—
    Before I'd been lang owre the main.

'Twas a blow to my hopes, for I never
　　Had my fond filial soul dispossess'd
Of that bright, happy plan of returning
　　And making the auld couple blest.

Yes, 'tis years since the decent auld couple
　　The way of all mortals did gang ;
In Ancrum kirkyaird, wi' my sister,
　　Already·they've rested for lang.
Now did I return to the auld place,
　　Sorely chang'd unto me a' would be ;
The forms so belov'd and so lovely
　　Nor in house nor in garden I'd see.

Baith outside and in I'd meet strangers,
　　And sair alterations I'd find ;
Oh ! I trow it is better the auld place
　　Remain as it is in my mind.
It's better to keep it in memory
　　As it was in the happy auld days,
Than to see't aiblins shapit and alter'd
　　By folk o' strange thoughts and new ways.

So I think oft in times o' reflection,
　　And I make up my mind to remain
In my country and place of adoption,
　　Nor to look on the auld place again.
Yet around the dear hame by the Teviot
　　Such flame-clouds of memory burn,
And a voice still doth speak from the Teviot—
　　" Return, thou auld wand'rer, return ! "

Ah ! is it the voice o' deid kinsfolk,
  Or is it the low, plaintive wail
O' the fresh simmer blast as 'tis sweeping
  Frae the hills adown fair Teviotdale?
I ken na'; but, oh ! 'mid my dreaming,
  That voice oft at midnight I hear,
And sair I am tempted to visit
  The scenes to my soul aye sae dear.

O hame ! where I on to young manhood
  Was nurtur'd in love warm and true;
Where I, mixing up labour and pleasure,
  Scarcely mark'd the bright days as they flew.
Let me look on't, howe'er it be alter'd,
  Let me see it ance mair ere I dee;
Though my darlings are a' deid and buried,
  The auld hame is still dear, dear to me.

Let me back, let me back to the Teviot,
  Though changes I'll see in ilk place;
The haunts and the paths so enchanting
  Of my boyhood and youth let me trace.
There's many a nook by the Teviot
  That to me in sad beauty will shine;
There's many a tree by the Teviot
  That can tell me a tale o' langsyne.

Let me visit auld Timpendean Castle,
  Let me muse o'er ilk grey, ruined wa';
Let me visit the bold crags o' Minto,
  Let me walk over proud Ruberslaw.

But oh, mair than a', let me visit
   The place where my parents repose,
By the lov'd one who died ere well tasting
   Life's banquets of pleasures and woes.

Ah ! there in the sweet simmer morning,
   Or when the mild evening dews fa',
All within the low sough o' Ale's wavelets,
   All the things of my past I'll reca'.
And oh, but I trow God's high lesson
   From my life's chequered pattern I'll learn ;
And truths, until then all unnoticed,
   Burning bright as the stars I'll discern.

JEDBURGH ABBEY.

CALL not the Ages mean, inglorious,
That left such noble monuments to us
As Jedburgh Abbey! Say not men, whose toil
Uprear'd such stately Gothic pile,
Had not in their souls' souls a God-like thought
Which ever strenuous outward wrought
Unto its fair material counterpart
In the rich realms of Art ;
Say not these builders did not ply
Their mighty tasks religiously ;
Say not they wrought not to the chime
Of the Eternal Harmonies sublime !
Thou massive pile, by massive spirits rear'd,
     Thy builders wrought
     Until their thought
In beautiful, enduring stone appear'd !

B

Oh ! relic so magnificent !
Oh ! venerable monument
Of palmy days long centuries past,
A boundless, rich significance thou hast
Unto my heart !   My heart deep homage pays
Unto the nobleness of ancient days,
Whereof thou art the august memorial !
Yes, thou through generations' rise and fall
Hast witnessed to our fathers' recognition
Of sacred Truth ; yea, to their blest endeavour
Upwards towards the Beatific Vision
In which the blessed dwell in peace for ever !
From thee, magnificent Ruin, looketh forth
The Eternal Aspiration of our race :
She who doth reach to things of loftiest worth,
The antitypes in God's own Dwelling Place !
Oh ! let me here the Heaven of Heavens extol
For that bright seraph of the human soul,
High Aspiration, who, on wings of flame,
Spurning our dross, salutes the home from whence we
       came !

Thou sacred house, uprear'd on sacred plan,
How eloquent art thou of God and Man !
Thy structure cruciform, how doth it show
Christ's and our human mystery of woe !
Yea, in thy threefold * unities we see
The symbol of the blessed Trinity !

---

* I refer to the triple breadth—aisle, nave, and aisle; the triple
length—nave, choir, sacrarium; and to the triple height—pierarch,
triforium, clerestory.

Beautiful Temple ! House of God !
  How fair wert thou in that old time
  When awe-struck Faith, with look sublime,
 Thy courts so lovely and so sacred trod !
Oh, still so fair ! and centuries gone o'er thee !
What must have been thy former glory ?
Would I might now depicture thee,
The joy of many a pilgrim heart
At home and far beyond the sea—
  The lovely House of Piety
  And generous Hospitality
That thou so many ages wert !
Would I might show thee in the old centuries
 Doing thy best religion to maintain,
And to attune to heavenly harmonies
 The wild, tumultuous lives of mortal men !
Would I might show thee when 'twas thine
 So largely men's deep needs to meet ;
When Grief still found in thee the Balm Divine ;
 When blest was Learning in thy calm retreat !
Or, might I for a space convey
Me back unto yon wond'rous day
When Alexander, Scotland's King,
Did his betroth'd to Jedward bring ;
And when the long procession up thy nave
Pass'd, while the organ music, wave on wave,
Roll'd forth with deep solemnity,
Yet with a burst of victory
Befitting the occasion, grand and brave !
Yea, might I paint the happy pair—
The monarch and his lady fair—

At thy high altar while the rite was done—
The sacred rite that made them one—
Might I reveal a little of the sheen,
The grandeur, and the pomp, of yonder old-world scene!

Thou venerable pile, had'st thou a tongue,
  Of many a revolution might'st thou tell :
Old systems that once seem'd like iron strong,
  Old customs that were deem'd unchangeable,
Old powers, ay, even old dynasties,
And all the ancient pageantries,
Hast thou outlasted! Since thou wert uprear'd
  What things have risen and had their day and fame,
And in the great time-torrent disappear'd,
  Nor left the thinnest phantom of a name!
What things have risen, and flourished, and then gone
Into the darkness of oblivion
While thou stood'st there! Oh, no! not Vandal wrath
  That smote thee; not the centuries
That have rush'd o'er thee with their wasting breath;
  Not these, not these, so potent agencies.
That do so much into oblivion bring,
Have made thee cease to be a glorious thing—
  A thing of wonder and of sacredness!
Old Gothic manhood, piety, and art,
  These with a quite peculiar faithfulness
  Look forth from thee; yea, these thou dost express,
As nought else can, to man's deep conscious heart!

THE MUIRLAND SHEPHERD'S WIDOW.

A TALE OF THE MUIRLANDS.

O, WHA among our classes high
   Wi' my dear Sandy could compare?
Or wha could be mair blest than I
   When I my Sandy's lot did share?

O, but he was a bonny lad,
   Sic manly beauty marked his face,
And sic a manly air he had,
   And wore the plaid wi' sic a grace.

What though he only was a herd
   Wi' a bit pack, he was sae dear
That I for him refus'd a laird—
   A laird wi' land and routh o' gear.

And sair my faither gloom'd on me,
   And a' my brethren ca'd me mad
To scorn a man o' high degree,
   And a' for a puir shepherd lad.

Ah, mony a thraw had I to thole,
   And mony a grief fell on my dear;
But love that's rooted in the soul
   Can stand the stroke o' winter-weir.

And strong and brave thro' a' was I,
   And strong and brave thro' a' was he;
And still we thought we could descry
   Bright days within futurity.

He gave to me the marriage ring,
    And I believ'd I'd be his wife;
And mickle joy to me did bring
    The thought o' happy married life.

I pictur'd out our wee bit cot
    In wild green glen embosomed fair;
And trow'd that humble tho' our lot,
    Ours would be bliss beyond compare.

Would not our hame the hale year round
    O' hames a very pattern be—
A place where true love could be found,
    A spot which Heaven well pleased might see?

O, I would keep it neat and clean,
    And he would light it wi' his smile;
And we would still be blythe and bien,
    Still rich in love and fruits o' toil.

And when my kindred should drap in,
    A heaven—nae less!—I trow'd they'd find;
And then they surely would begin,
    If not before, to change their mind.

They'd see that at the least my choice
    Had fall'n on ane right gude and leal,
And O my father would rejoice
    That it had a' turn'd out sae weel.

And we his blessing then would get—
    The blessing of a father dear—
And in a trice we would forget
    That he had e'er been dour and sweir.

And truly it had a' turned out
    Even as I'd dream'd, even as I'd thought;
Ah, Providence without a doubt
    For us had plann'd, for us had wrought.

I wedded him I fondly loved,
    And ere lang time had o'er us gane
Faither and brethren had approved
    Wi' their hale hearts the step I'd ta'en.

And in all fortunes I must say,
    While looking back upon my life,
That I joy's summit reached that day
    When I became my Sandy's wife!

Our house was just a but-an'-ben,
    But pleas'd was I as mistress there,
For Sandy was the wale o' men,
    And I wi' him had ne'er a care.

Blythely he went baith out and in,
    A man, 'twas clear, o' gladsome mind;
And to the last 'twas his to win
    Gowden opinions frae his kind.

In a' gude ways he bore the bell,
    As weel as for his manly might;
And wi' my ain gudeman to dwell
    It was, I vouch, a true delight.

But now my sad, sad tale:—His wife
    I'd been but barely towmonds twa,
When dearest Sandy lost his life
    Among the driving, pouthery snaw.

O weel I mind that fatal day !
   When Sandy op'd at morn the door,
'Twas light enough to see there lay
   A gryming slight wide o'er the muir.

Gaily he gaed away that morn,
   Gaily as wont that day began ;
Little I thought he'd ne'er return
   Alive—O my beloved young man !

'Twas morning still when frae the lift
   The tempest broke o'er muir and hill
And what wi' thickening snaws and drift,
   'Twas threatening many a yowe to kill.

Sudden it came, and wildly fierce,
   Soon it was roaring all abroad ;
Its sound my very soul did pierce,
   I couldna' guess what it might bode.

I just had been wi' baking thrang,
   The girdle just had set away,
When in the door blew wi' a bang,
   The house was like being blawn away !

I seized the door, and ga'e a look
   To the outside—how dark the gloom !
Heaven, earth, my heart, and a' things shook
   Wi' the loud tempest's dismal boom !

Quick, quick I steek'd the door—turn'd in,
   And at the winnock took a seat,
And, looking at the winnock-pane,
   I broke into a death-cauld sweat.

Strange, awsome fears did me o'erpower;
  "What if my dear gudeman," I cried,
"Should now be caught upon the muir,
  Or on the hill's bleak open side?

"Doubtless he marked the coming storm,
  And hurried on his flock to save—
O what if now his manly form
  Be sinking in a snowy grave?"

And Fancy 'gan to represent
  Him battling with the driving blast;
I saw him wrestling there, till spent
  Wi' toil he sank, and a' was past.

But with my fears anon I strove,
  Anon by earnest prayer I gave
The cherished object of my love
  Unto that God who's strong to save.

"Father and God!" I loudly cried,
  "Save—for thou canst—my ain gudeman!
Him in Thine ain hand's hollow hide
  Until the blast be overblawn!"

And while I pray'd, my fierce heart-pain,
  My sair solicitude, seem'd o'er;
But soon 'twas wakened up again
  By the mad storm's tumultuous roar.

So through the day in anxious state
  I sat till it was afternoon;
And then the storm began to abate,
  Till by and by the wind was doon.

But O the tumult of my heart
  Was not a whit diminishèd;
Nay, now the thought came like a dart—
  "Out in the snow thy love lies dead!"

"Out in the snow thy love lies dead!"
  Was that a voice of ghostly tone
That spoke the words? I shook wi' dread,
  Yet still sat waiting, waiting on.

Then twa o'clock I heard; then three
  Chappin'; and still nae Sandy came;
"O God!" I cried, "alive to me
  Sandy, I fear, will ne'er come hame."

Then something seemed to force me forth,
  Something that wouldna be said nay;
And o'er a white and wintry earth
  I took my toilsome, painful way.

Onward, still onward, did I gang;
  Now here, now there, now everywhere;
On through the snaw, wi' efforts strang,
  Wi' efforts prompted by despair.

At length, a bittie on, I saw
  An object—O, what could it be?—
An object black as ony craw,
  And but craw size unto the e'e.

And drawing nearer I could tell
  It was his dog, his Rover gude:
O, pitying Heaven! I knew full well
  Near what it was that Rover stude.

A something surely in me said
   'Twas watching by his master's form;
His master's form now cauld and dead,
   Made lifeless by the cruel storm.

And wi' a cry, and wi' a bound,
   In desperation on I ran;
I ken nae mair—O I was found
   Beside my lov'd, my deid young man.

I there was found, cauld as if Death
   Had also slain and endit me,
And Rover watching o'er us baith,
   As faithfu' as a dog could be.

Yes, it was a' as I hae said;
   And when to consciousness I came,
I found me helpless and in bed,
   In bed in my death-shadow'd hame.

I found that I for weeks had there
   In a delirious fever been,
And that my Sandy never mair
   Would cheer for me this mortal scene.

Ah, while I tell this waesome tale,
   His noble dog, his Rover's near,
We baith together now bewail
   Our faithful friend, our master dear.

Ah, Rover! Rover! dinna lift
   Upon me sic a waesome e'e!
Ye mind me o' the stormy drift,
   And a' the sad, sad tragedy.

O dinna gar me greet! I ken
　　The warld wi' us is changèd sair:
I ken I've lost the wale o' men—
　　Yes, there, O there's his empty chair!

And there's his checkit plaidie fine,
　　And there's his bannet, staff, and a';
O that belov'd young man o' mine
　　That perish'd 'mang the swirling snaw!

THE EMIGRANT'S RETURN TO THE RULE.

'TWAS moonlight! not a leaf did stir
　　Within the balmy wood,
When on thy bridge, fair Bonchester,
　　An aged wanderer stood.

Once full of majesty and strength
　　Had surely been his form,
Though now 'twas bent, as it at length
　　Had yielded to life's storm.

His hair was snowy; you could trace
　　Its youthful hue no more;
His venerable furrow'd face
　　With grief was shaded o'er.

'Twas shaded o'er—a spirit fraught
　　With lasting grief it spoke;
Yet once, as he of boyhood thought,
　　A splendour o'er it broke.

Now seem'd he gazing on the Rule,
　His own dear native stream ;
Yet, oh, he saw it not : his soul
　Was holden in a dream.

Up, up the chequer'd flood of years,
　As on the wind, he flew,
Till the old Time's face, in its young grace
　And careless mirth, he knew.

Again he liv'd his boyhood o'er ;
　Once more by bonnie Rule
He joined the merry, lusty roar
　Of imps let loose from school.

Again the glassy pool he tried
　What time the sun was high ;
Again in naked races vied
　Till he was warm and dry.

Once more he liv'd the golden days
　When he, in dreams, would climb,
Like pilgrim, up romantic ways
　To man's estate sublime.

Again he ardently desir'd
　A stalwart man to be,
For glowing tales his fancy fir'd
　Of lands beyond the sea.

Then one in beauty's tender bloom
　Arose within his thought ;
Even she, the fair young bride, with whom
　He foreign lands had sought.

Autumnal glory lit the shade,
  The barley ear was full,
When he and his fair Marion bade
  Adieu to bonnie Rule.

How much since then had come and gone!
  'Twas fifty years ago;
He seem'd like pine-tree, old and lone,
  Waiting the woodman's blow.

And this thought came now full suddenly
  And chilly o'er his heart,
And from his blissful reverie
  He woke up with a start.

Yes, he was old, and lone, and bare,
  Just like an aged tree
That shivers alone in the northern air
  On a bare acclivity.

For he had seen his Marion true
  Laid in a foreign grave;
Had seen her beauteous issue, too,
  Sink down, and could not save.

And now unto his native place
  Had he return'd, to find
That there remained of him no trace
  Within a living mind.

He had eager look'd through the auld kirkyaird,
  To each hamlet home had gone;
Ah! not one kinsman Death had spared,
  Of former friends but one:

One who had stood in Time's cold blast
   Till shrivell'd, deaf, and blind,
And so benumb'd in thought, the past
   Was buried out of mind.

Ah! now into the wanderer's e'e
   Started some briny tears,
While he sadly thought on the changes wrought
   In fifty weary years.

Rule's moonlight stream now bending o'er,
   His heart to breaking full,
" Fair scenes," he sighed, " bloom as of yore,
   Flow on, thou crystal Rule;

" Your loveliness no longer cheers,
   It stirs but thoughts of pain;
For, oh, the friends of other years
   Can ne'er come back again.

" Again to that far land I'll go
   Where sleeps my Marion dear,
Where rest mine offspring—I shall know
   Rest there; but, oh, not here.

" Oh, there from life's long thrall set free,
   My last repose I'll find;
And parted friends at length shall be
   In blest reunion join'd."

THE SPRING O' THE YEAR.

'Tis Winter bauld; on roaring blasts
    Wide fly the sheeted snaws;
The sheep crouch in their stells; the birds
    Cower deep intil the shaws.
But let grim Winter rage his warst,
    Sweet Hope our hearts will cheer
Wi' visions o' that heavenly time,
    The Spring o' the year.

O why, gudewife, hae I been wud
    In these wild Winter days,
Still threapin' that the snaws hae put
    The capstane on our waes?
Our mailin, true, has done but ill,
    And wasted our bit gear;
Yet some remede may wait us in
    The Spring o' the year.

Be that or no! this comfort's ours:
    It never can be said
That we have an unworthy part
    Among our fellows played.
Gudewife! we've done the honest thing;
    'Tis ken'd baith far and near;
And we'll haud up our heads and wait
    The Spring o' the year.

Why, why on seas of anxious strife
  Have I been toss'd about?
Naked into the world we came,
  And naked we'll gang out.
And as our day our strength shall be :
  Awa' wi' coward fear!
Awa' wi' a' that hides from sight
  The Spring o' the year !

O shame that we should let the world
  E'er spoil our heart's fine tune !
It's no worth while; the youngest o's
  Will see an end o't soon.
And come what may, the Lord still shields
  His folk frae winter's weir ;
And gi'es to a' for solace sweet
  The Spring o' the year.

Cheer up, gudewife, I've vow'd a vow,
  And I will ne'er go back :
I'll do my best, and trust the Lord
  To save us going to wrack.
Whate'er befa', I thro' the world
  Will calmly onward steer,
Nor be denied the solace o'
  The Spring o' the year.

The Spring o' the year, when hush'd
  Are Winter's brattling storms,
When God the miracle of life
  On every hand performs.

C

O precious, precious recompense
  For the Winter lang and drear,
Nature's rejuvenating time,
  The Spring o' the year.

Yes, Winter's reign will soon be o'er ;
  Soon, soon a charmèd earth,
As if beneath a seraph's kiss,
  Will bud and blossom forth.
The saft green gerse will cleed the braes,
  The burnies ripple clear ;
And mickle joy we'll hae when comes
  The Spring o' the year.

We'll mark the primrose that now lies
  Forsaken in its tomb ;
We'll see the hawthorn, now sae bare,
  Burst in a cloud of bloom.
The violet we shall seek and find,
  Still wet wi' Night's pure tear,
All in that lovely, tender time,
  The Spring o' the year.

We'll see the lambs upon the braes
  Around their dams at play ;
And oh, I doubtna' but we'll be
  As blythe in heart as they.
And blackbirds frae the forest cleugh
  Will shout, " Our bridal's here ! "
All in that happy, heavenly time,
  The Spring o' the year,

And thro' the leelang vernal day
　Thou'lt still be at my side ;
And, like some mountain burnie's waves,
　Our thoughts will onward glide.
And I will tell my heart's fond tale,
　And surely thine I'll hear,
As when we walk'd all in yon bright,
　Bright Spring o' the year.

HOWDEN BURN.

Now Nature's clad in garments gay,
And sweet it is on bank and brae ;
And oh, so sweet by Howden Burn,
That there even mortal foes might iearn
　　To live in happy union.

There on the braes the little lambs
Gambol around their sober dams,
While 'mong the blooming hawthorn sprays
The wild birds vow in simple lays
　　To live in happy union.

Come, Mary, in the summer ray
Adown the glen let's take our way,
'Twixt braes bedeck'd with furze and fern ;
Come, let us walk by Howden Burn,
　　And live in happy union.

Yes, come! we'll track the burnie's thread,
The winding sheep-paths we will tread,
And climb the braes so steep and high,
And still 'twill be our dearest joy
. To live in happy union.

Yes, come! we here and there will go
As Fancy leads, and still will know
. Rest, sweetest rest, from worldly strife;
Yea, to the angel-side of life
            Attain thro' happy union.

Yes, come! and by yon bonnie burn
We for earth's better day will yearn;
The day when men shall all agree,
And the blue heavens look down and see
            The world's great social union.

MY FATHER'S DEATH.

When, like richest, heavenly donor, Spring was giving gifts
    to earth;
When the forests, glens, and muirlands rang with high
    triumphal mirth;
Then, as if on beauty's threshold, lay my venerable sire,
In his eyes a dying longing—in his breast a dying fire.

Oh, these mornings! bright spring mornings! as if heaven
    were open wide,
In they came upon us, streaming, each a great celestial
    tide;

Then, as at a given signal, would the woods their voices
    raise,
And with merle and with linnet oft we vied in songs ot
    praise.

Often, too, when sank night's shadows, and the wild-bird's
    hymn grew faint,
We would sing some holy anthem suitable to dying
    saint.
In the sanctuary of sorrow we made rare sweet
    melody,
For our notes were emanations from the heart's deep
    swelling sea.

Oh, these holy, last communings! all too sacred they for
    speech—
Nay, their depths and elevations words of mine could never
    reach.
Ever bow'd he to the Highest, ever with a strength
    sublime
Said he—"Lord, I'm only waiting, only waiting Thy good
    time."

And, while waiting, look'd he daily from his chamber
    window forth,
And he thought that he had never seen such beauty in the
    earth.
Glory fill'd him, glory thrill'd him, while on the green earth
    he gaz'd,
For the flow'rs and grass with glory on his dying vision
    blaz'd.

Thus he watch'd, and daily waited; long it was ere death
    could claim
The inevitable tribute, his so strong and massive frame.
Came the end after this manner:—Death had struggled hard
    with Life
One long night, and with the morning came a lulling of the
    strife.

Weary then and faint, he rested his poor head upon my hands,
And I whisper'd—"Lo! he sleepeth; sleep his feeble state
    demands."
'Twas just then, 'mid ominous silence, I beheld with bated
    breath,
On his cheek a ghastly pallor, and I said—"Can this be
    death?"

Yes, 'twas death! the strange, last milestone that we come
    to, one by one;
He had passed it—all was over; he had been, and done,
    and gone!
He, the man of sense and courage, and of rarest courteous
    grace,
Had departed; nor would any fill for us his empty place.

Man 'mong men wert thou, my father; and the seeing at a
    glance
Saw in thee a king of labour, born to conquer circumstance.
And thou didst both do and conquer; and a generous,
    fruitful tree
Thou didst flourish here for many—thou didst flourish here
    for me.

Yes ! thou wert both wise and valiant, apt to plan and apt
    to do ;
Purposing, and in thy manhood carrying thy purpose
    through.
Mark'd by great things, and by greater was thine arduous
    course on earth ;
And, like all things that are grandest, deep and silent was
    thy worth.

THE FLOWER OF RULE.

AMONG the verdant wilds o' Rule
    She dwelt, a maid refin'd,
Whose work was in the hamlet school
    To build the infant mind.

There was not in the countryside
    A maid of finer grace ;
And ne'er, methinks, have you espied
    One with more speaking face.

In the hero-element of hope
    She mov'd all unconfin'd,
And her form, so stately towering up,
    Well index'd forth her mind.

She was as fair as lily white,
    Well nurs'd with sun and show'rs ;
And, oh, upon her shone a light
    From a brighter world than ours.

She made the waste life beautiful,
  As if with living streams;
And still she shone by crystal Rule
  As in the light of dreams.

She was my lily; every day
  I pass'd by where.she dwelt;
And never did I pass that way
  But wondrous things I felt.

I oft call'd reason to my aid,
  And with my feelings strove;
But still I lov'd the beauteous maid
  With an impassion'd love.

What time the day's soft-dying grace
  Lay on the hill and grove,
All in the heaven of her face
  I told my tale of love.

With fears my heart's fond tale I told,
  For how could I opine
That unto me she would unfold
  A tale as warm as mine?

Spring in embroider'd robes stood nigh,
  Like maiden in her pride,
And kiss'd her bonnie brow, while I
  Did claim her as my bride.

The sky, all bright with rainbow lines,
  Now bent like God's hand o'er us;
And God's bright world, that we might choose,
  Was lying all before us.

But, ah! too soon I saw her fade,
  Too soon death's dews, so chilly,
Fell on her; and she bow'd her head,
  My own pale, dying lily.

She died! the good, the young, the fair;
  But not by crystal Rule;
Yet still, in dreams, I see her there,
  In her dear hamlet school.

Oh, whereso'er I roam I yearn
  For the dear scenes of Rule,
And still my thoughts, like exiles, turn
  Unto her hamlet school.

MY MITHER'S HAME.

WHAT is the truest thing on earth
  That a true son of man can name?
What is the soil of manly worth?
  Oh! is it not a mither's hame?
My mither was a mither true,
  As e'er inspir'd a filial flame;
And, oh! the blessings werena few
  That met ye in my mither's hame.

Palatial grandeur wasna there,
  Nor greatness wi' its cumbrous load;
But honest souls found something mair—
  They found the noblest work of God:

They found a large and loving heart,
  A gifted woman, void of blame;
They found life's grand and glorious part
  Abiding in my mither's hame.

I see her yet, I see her yet,
  The woman of the sterling mind,
The brave, true lady every whit,
  The ornament of womankind!
Again do I my witness gie,
  That whatsoever went or came,
Life's beauty, life's fine dignity,
  Still met me in my mither's hame.

O vanish'd gude! thou comes na back!
  And at her door nae mair I'll ca'
To hae her crack, and to partak'
  O' her pot-luck sae guid and braw.
Nae mair will I, when dark my lot,
  Her kind maternal solace claim;
Nor as unto a shelter'd spot
  Betake me to my mither's hame.

Oh! how the auld things pass away!
  There's naething in the world can last;
All things maun sune or late decay,
  And yield to Time's resistless blast.
But, oh! beyond yon dreary goal
  Fond Love re-trims her deathless flame,
And something says within my soul
  That there is now my mither's hame!

THE WILD BRACKEN GLEN.

WHEN beauty walks forth, of the dawn newly born,
When fresh are the dews and the scents of the morn,
When each leaf in the wood and each flower on the sod
Is alive, as if touch'd by the finger of God,
  Oh, then, let me go
  Where the streamlet sings low,
Athreading with silver the wild bracken glen.

Then shimmering and glimmering, the glen, dew-impearl'd,
Is fair as a glimpse of a new Eden world;
And the kine softer browse by the morning-struck stream,
And life is all wrapp'd in a calm blessed dream,
  Where the primroses blow,
  And the streamlet sings low,
Athreading with silver the wild bracken glen.

And when the last bleatings have died far away,
And deep starry silence extendeth her sway;
When the great heart of Nature is throbbing for God,
And we feel deep, mysterious sighings abroad,
  Oh, then, let me go
  Where the streamlet sings low,
Athreading with silver the wild bracken glen.

For the wild bracken glen, when God's fingers nnroll
That evangel of beauty, the night's starry scroll,
Is a temple of God, an all-sacred retreat,
And the toil-worn may rest at the Deity's feet,
  Where the primroses blow,
  And the streamlet sings low,
Athreading with silver the wild bracken glen.

OH, IT'S UP THROUGH JED-FOREST.

OH, it's up through Jed-forest, to meet 'mong the foremost
　The bright blushing spring, bonnie Marion hied;
And, indeed, she did meet her; and, indeed, she did greet
　　her;
　But the spring miss'd a friend frae poor Marion's side.
As lovely as ever, by Jed's crystal river,
　Was the spring's lovely face; yet, tho' a' things were
　　braw,
Marion's griefs they were flowing, and, o'er a bank bowing,
　In Jed's running waters she let her tears fa'. ·

"Oh, John," cried the maiden, "my heart it is laden
　Wi' dule and wi' care—all my joy it is fled;
By thee I'm forsaken, and spring canna waken
　The hopes I ance felt on the banks o' the Jed.
I ance was the fairest—I ance was the dearest;
　But my life, like a flower, is now bow'd to the grave:
Come, Death, do thou slay me! Come, Death, do thou
　　lay me
　Asleep, oh, for ever, by Jed's crystal wave!"

Oh, it's up through Jed-forest! nae mair 'mong the foremost,
　For anither young spring will poor Marion hie;
It still is but simmer, still green is the timmer,
　But low, in deep silence, the fairest doth lie.
Sing, sing, thou dear river! yes, sing on for ever!
　Or hoarsely, by bank and by scaur, onward roar!
Thou canst not awaken whom sorrow hath taken;
　Full soundly she sleeps, and will waken no more!

OH, WERE WE IN YON BONNIE GLEN.

Oh, were we in yon bonnie glen,
Sae far away frae haunts o' men ;
Oh, were we in yon bonnie glen,
And deep into its flowery den,
Where jouks and sings the little wren ;
Oh, there, I trow, ye sune wad ken
   How dearly do I love thee.

It's oh, were mine a monarch's crown,
Even at thy feet I'd lay it down ;
It's oh, were mine a monarch's crown,
I'd pass the belles in yonder town,
And seek ye in life's valley lowne,
And take thee in thy plaidin' gown,
   Sae dearly do I love thee.

WOLFELEE.

Oh, green Wolfelee, still unto thee
   I turn with feelings tender ;
For thou, to me, for ever art
   All bath'd in morning splendour.

I see thee still in mantle woven
   Of dews and sunbeams lying ;
And, oh, as for a promis'd land,
   For thee I still am sighing.

Oh, thou art ever in my dreams,
  Like some fair shining Eden;
And I long to be in thee, Wolfelee,
  What time thy roses redden.

I long to rove thy green retreats,
  'Neath Fancy's kind direction,
And to see in every flower and tree
  An object of affection.

I long, while forests' hearts are full
  Of dearest loves and pleasures,
To walk adown by bonnie Rule,
  And view the summer's treasures.

Oh, green Wolfelee, might I in thee
  But see the young lambs gambol,
And feel the joyful liberty
  Of things so fair and humble!

And might I gang unto thy kirk—
  I and my friends together—
Along the accustom'd shady way
  In the Sabbatic weather!

But why these accents of my heart?
  Oh, why this ceaseless yearning?
Oh, green Wolfelee, now unto thee,
  For me, is no returning.

I must not go to thy green retreats,
  Nor walk by Rule's fair river;
For the friends of auld lang syne are gone,
  And they'll come back, oh, never!

WOLFELEE STILL REMEMBER'D.

'Tis twelve long years since last I stray'd
 Through thy retreats, Wolfelee,
Yet never has my heart been dead
 One moment unto thee.

Still exile-like to thee I've turned ;
 Yea, when I've furthest been
Away from thee, I've fondliest yearn'd
 For thy retreats so green.

The glory of old summers gone,
 Still, still, Wolfelee I've seen,
Like some fine fairy mantle, thrown
 O'er thy retreats so green.

Yea, has not busy Fancy made
 Thee shine in hues more bright
Than brightest hues in thee display'd
 At summer's dazzling height ?

O have I not oft pictur'd thee
 As some fair land of rest,
Where yet the friends long lost to me
 Would take me to their breast ?

As some fair land of rest, where I
 My treasures left behind ;
Some Eden-scene where by and by
 I these again might find ?

Have I not felt as if to thee
　　One day I back might come,
And find, just as it wont to be,
　　My dear remember'd home?

As if I yet in thee might find,
　　Around the wonted board,
The old joy of heart, the old peace of mind
　　Abundantly restor'd?

Vain dreams! Ah, did I seek in thee
　　The things I once enjoy'd,
My poor illusion then would be
　　Too mis'rably destroy'd.

Vain dreams! this heart that restless beats.
　　And heaves with longing sore,
Would break within thy green retreats,
　　Would break by Rule's fair shore.

To thee I may not come again,
　　O lov'd, O fair Wolfelee;
Yet in my soul for aye remain
　　A beauteous memory!

Still in fine robes of heavenly light
　　For me, for me be dress'd;
Still seem an Eden calm and bright,
　　Where I may yet find rest!

Still would I cheer life's cloudy way
　　With many a radiant view;
And dream (what harm?) that yet I may
　　My brightest hours renew!

JEANNIE GRAY.

THE wild bird sang sweet at the break o' the morning,
    The gowan bloom'd fair i' the spring o' the year,
When weary frae lang years o' wandering, returning,
    I sought the blue hills, to my heart aye sae dear.
I gaed to the braes where, beside the sweet Yarrow,
    I tented my lambs through the blythe summer day ;
And doon the lang glen, wi' my heart fu' o' sorrow,
    I lookit for Jeannie, my sweet Jeannie Gray.

I gaed to the spot where our young loves were plighted,
    The lintie sang sweetly as ever to me,
And through the blue hills the bright morning beams lighted
    My Jeannie's dear hame, 'neath the bonnie haw tree.
I gaed to her hame—oh, 'twas cauld and forsaken,
    The thistle had sprung where the warm hearthstane lay ;
And the robin was chirpin', as if to awaken,
    Frae death's early slumbers, my sweet Jeannie Gray.

I spier'd a herd laddie I met on the mountain,
    Yet naething of Jeannie he tauld unto me ;
I spier'd a young maiden wha sang by the fountain,
    But only she wipit the tear frae her e'e.
At last I sat doon, where a bird, strangely flitting,
    Rang out a wild story o' dule and o' wae ;
Ah ! there she was lying, and there, lanely sitting,
    I grat o'er the grave o' my sweet Jeannie Gray.

———

D

TO MY BOY RECOVERING FROM SICKNESS.

AWAKE, bonnie boy; now thy sickness is past,
And so, thank kind Heaven! is the cold cutting blast:
Now blows, softly blows the sweet south-western wind,
And the bright bonnie Spring leaves grim Winter behind.
The snowdrop and crocus have long ago blossom'd,
And now in the dells and the valleys embosom'd
The primrose is blooming, and in each woodway
The windflow'r and sorrel their bright specks display.
The violet, too, and the speedwell are springing,
And the foxglove her dainty bells soon will be ringing;
'Tis also the time of the singing of birds—
Oh, might we translate their sweet songs into words!
The cuckoo has long to the glad Spring been calling,
Her voice, like a maiden's voice, rising and falling;
The curlew and lapwing are heard on the moors,
And high, at heaven's portals, the skylark adores.
And the greenwood is vocal and blythesome; for in it
Are the thrush and the mavis, and blackbird and linnet:
Arouse thee, my boy, on this bonnie Spring day,
To our dear pretty farmhouse we'll hie us away.
And there flowing tankards of milk I will give thee,
And butter, and eggs, and cream-cakes to revive thee;
And thou, bonnie boy, on the strength of that meat,
Wilt with me spend the day all in wanderings sweet.
And shouldst thou e'er falter, for rest we will tarry,
Or o'er bank and o'er brae shoulder-high thee I'll carry;
And the sweet vernal air and the blythe vernal voices,
(Oh, now is the season great Nature rejoices!)

And the sun sparkling bright through the light forest greenery,
And all the fine changes of beautiful scenery—
These, O my dear boy, these will wholly restore thee
To childhood's pure health, and fine gladness and glory.
Come away! now enough of the doctor's drug-mysteries;
Country sunshine and air will do more than dispensaries;
Physician and medicine at once is kind Nature
For boy, and for man, and for every poor creature.
Come away to the country; oh! come, bonnie boy,
And drink at the fountains of health, strength, and joy!

THOUGHTS AT MY MOTHER'S GRAVE.

Now night her curtain o'er the earth has spread,
   And slow the moon mounts up the cloudy sky;
And from deep musings on the banks of Jed,
   My mother, at thy grave, lo! here am I.

And liest thou low? Oh, liest thou here so low,
   Thou who wert mother, friend, and guide to me;
Thou whose large heart did with such feelings glow
   As did do honour to humanity?

Yes, thou art gone! The last beloved link
   That bound me to a not unsacred past
Is broken now; and oh, with tears, I think
   Of all thou wert to me from first to last.

While thou couldst think at all, of me thou thought'st;
   While thou couldst do, thou still for me didst do;
From first to last my weal thou fondly sought'st,
   And brightest blessings on my path didst strew.

Thy love to me was like a fountain clear
    Which suns can ne'er exhaust, nor frosts arrest ;
Some tree of Paradise that all the year
    At once with pleasant flowers and fruits is dress'd.

Nor idly do I say thou mightst have shone—
    How great thine early possibilities !
Yea, to the last thy nature had the tone
    And grandeur of the higher harmonies.

But happiness enough it was for thee
    To live a loving human life on earth ;
To walk in meekness and integrity
    Along the common path of humble worth.

The pomp of state, the glory of the great,
    The splendour that doth strike the vulgar blind,
The applause that doth on earth's successful wait—
    Thy heart did leave such baubles far behind.

To be as thy good parents here had been —
    This was thy wish ; and that thou wert no less
In power and gift to bless this human scene—
    This, this, I say, was even our happiness.

No sinecure 'twas given thee here to find—
    Cares, toils amany to thy lot did fall ;
But with a noble, independent mind
    Thou didst acquit thyself amid them all.

Thou wert the child of many prayers ; and trust
    Hadst thou in an all-ruling Providence ;
And didst fare on, a woman brave and just,
    Full of fine humour and of common-sense.

Farewell! thy course thou hast right bravely run ;
   Thy toils are ended, and thy warfare's o'er ;
And thou hast gone to where the Eternal Sun
   Permits to thee no cloud, no sorrow more.

Oh, may I meet thee there !—far from the strife
   And turmoil of this transient mortal state ;
May we together share that ample life
   To which the just must come or soon or late !

OLD PLACES REVISITED.

ONCE more among the hills I roam,
   Where dwelt the fairest of the fair ;
   And though no more I'll find her there,
Yet must I seek the dear hill-home.

Nor only to the lov'd hill-home
   Must I now go ; but to the place
   Where bright she shone in maiden grace :—
But now to the hill-home I've come.

Here is the farm-house where we spent
   The blissfulest first-married years—
   The house the saintliest dead endears—
To which she hath a glory lent.

'Twas here she dwelt ; and, oh, she made
   A palace of a poor abode :
   Here we were happy ; here to God
We, morn and even, our homage paid.

Here, too, the garden where she stray'd ;
  Where holy thought within her woke,
  Or when the ruddy morning broke,
Or when the day began to fade.

Oh, privileg'd, long-vanish'd years,
  Again I know ye flowing past ;
  Strange splendours now ye on me cast,
And stir in me the fount of tears.

And here's the house, amid the pines,
  Where she, a lovely maiden, shone—
  'Twas pretty in the years long gone—
Now all in solemn light it shines.

Oh, beauteous dwelling !—her abode,
  Where all was neat and orderly—
  Where all her life was melody—
It was to me a House of God.

Here, too, the pleasant, spacious school,
  Where she young ductile spirits taught
  To read and think, and, as they ought,
Strive toward the moral beautiful.

Oh, privileg'd, long-vanish'd years !
  Again I know ye flowing past ;
  Strange splendours now ye on me cast,
And stir in me the fount of tears.

WHEN HAIRSTS HAE A'.

WHEN hairsts hae a' been gather'd in,
   And snaws on flichtering blasts are swirl'd ;
When sangs, and cracks, and blythesome din
   At firesides mak' a heartsome world—
Oh, then thy blythesome voice is miss'd,
   Thine empty chair I start to see,
And deeply sigh o'er a' the joy
   That faded and that died wi' thee.

When Spring, frae blooming southran bow'rs,
   Comes in wi' herald-cuckoos gay,
And curlews cry o'er heathery moors,
   And laverocks soar and sing away—
Oh, then thy mountain sangs are miss'd
   On rugged hills, by fountain sheen,
And a' the mirth o' God's green earth
   But tells o' that whilk ance has been.

When Simmer hings o'er thy bow'r-door
   The red, red rose, sae fair to see,
And leafy forest-arches pour
   Sweet showers o' merry minstrelsy—
Oh, then thy wud-notes wild are miss'd,
   And, oh, the rose I wont to pu'
May deck nae mair thy raven hair,
   Or vie wi' thy soft cheeks' rose-hue.

When Autumn comes, so red and sere,
   And Beauty's wrecks o'er earth are strown ;
When, 'mid the remnants o' the year,
   The wild-bird's note grows sad and lone—

Oh, then thy blythesome voice is miss'd,
  And phantom-shadows o'er me brood
Sae mournfully, they gar me sigh
  For Winter's storms and whirlwinds rude.

MEMORIAL OF A MIDSUMMER DAY IN 1888.

TO MR. AND MRS. M——, GLEN EDEN VILLA, ST. BOSWELL'S.

AMONG glad days, that backward smile
  With a rare enchanting power,
Must rank yon summer day we spent
  In sweet Glen Eden's bower.

O hostess kind, thy presence mild,
  Thy noble, winning ways ;
Thy fine heart-warmth, thy various gifts—
  These quite surpass my praise.

I need not say that thou dost make
  The Eden scene more fair ;
Nor that in thought I'll see thee still
  A ministering angel there.

I need not say that thou'rt a type
  Of noblest matron-worth ;
Nor that 'tis women of thy mark
  That make true heavens on earth.

Lovely thou in thy flowery nook,
   Thine own dear home, dost shine;
The glory meek, the grace subdu'd
   Of happy age is thine.

And thou, dear venerable host,
   Of thee what shall I say?
The sunshine of thy heart did well
   Befit yon summer day.

And oft in thought on the Braeheads,
   Where thou our steps didst lead,
I'll hear thy happy memories blend
   With the deep voice of Tweed.

And when I meet a mutual friend,
   To him or her I'll tell
How in fine gifted, humorous speech,
   Thou still dost bear the bell.

And should some say that Scottish wit
   Has lost its pristine power,
I'll point them on to Boswell's green,
   And sweet Glen Eden's bower.

I'll point them there. Not eighty years
   Of joy and sorrow blent
Have dulled thy wit and humorous life,
   Thou " old man eloquent."

I'll point them there. In thine old place
   Thou sittest brave and grand;
No common man—but even a king
   Within our Borderland.

Thou sittest there ; there wilt thou sit,
    Fresh-hearted to the last ;
Yea, brimming o'er with memories
    And stories of the past.

Yes, 'mong glad days, that backward smile
    With a rare enchanting power,
Must rank yon summer's day we spent
    In sweet Glen Eden's bower.

Adieu ! old friends, adieu ! Heaven still
    Rich blessings on you shower !
And many a year yet may you see
    In sweet Glen Eden's bower.

And when at length it comes you must
    Lay down your mortal load,
Soft may you fall asleep upon
    The bosom of your God !

TEVIOTSIDE.

O BUT we were fu' blythe and glad
    By bonnie Teviotside ;
Yea, pleasures there as fine we had
    As can to man betide ;
We've been unblest 'mid lovely scenes,
In spite o' routh o' ways and means,
But oh, we felt like kings and queens
    By bonnie Teviotside.

It was na' we were rich and braw
    By bonnie Teviotside;
Our haddin' there, indeed, was sma',
    Our needs were just supplied.
Yet, having learn'd to be content
Wi' what o' gude Heaven kindly sent,
Right happy were the days we spent
    By bonnie Teviotside.

Oh, my wife her house did nobly rule
    By bonnie Teviotside;
And by no fashionable school
    We in the least were tied;
A noble freedom we enjoy'd,
And our time as best we could employ'd,
And felt within no aching void
    By bonnie Teviotside.

And so fresh was aye our bairnies' glee
    By bonnie Teviotside,
And the Muse so kindly looked on me,
    That when my harp I tried,
Before I wist the uprising thought
I into beauteous forms had wrought,
The golden numbers came unsought
    By bonnie Teviotside.

Dear Nature's lovely realms were ours
    By bonnie Teviotside,
And 'mong the fields and trees and flowers
    'Twas bliss to wander wide.

And the larks were up wi' morning light,
And, far into the summer night,
To us they minister'd delight
    By bonnie Teviotside.

And 'twas sweet to mark the shepherd-boy
    By bonnie Teviotside;
Yea, on the haughs it was a joy
    For hours wi' him to abide;
And the noble kine, as in a dream,
Would stand midway in Teviot's stream,
And, oh, like heaven it all would seem
    By bonnie Teviotside.

And by steading bien and castle grey,
    On bonnie Teviotside,
'Twas grand to wander far away
    Just as the Muse might guide;
And grand it was of deeds to tell
That in the ancient time befell,
Of Scottish might that bore the bell
    By bonnie Teviotside.

Oh, the days are aye to memory dear
    We spent by Teviotside;
The days which aye like wavelets clear
    Did o'er us sweetly glide;
The Simmer days, so sweet and warm,
And the days when Autumn's golden charm
Was lying all o'er grove and farm
    By bonnie Teviotside.

And hearts all fresh with heavenly dew
    We found by Teviotside;
Hearts to the Godlike and the True,
    As a' might see, allied;
And I 'mong these had made abode,
If it had been the will of God,
Till I had gone the appointed road
    By bonnie Teviotside.

But now I've said a long farewell
    To bonnie Teviotside;
I've pu'd, perhaps, my last blue bell
    By Teviot's silver tide;
Yet if I should return again,
I'll surely feel, wi' deep heart-pain,
The loss of some who once were fain
    By bonnie Teviotstde.

POEM WRITTEN ON THE OCCASION OF THE LAYING OF THE MEMORIAL-STONE OF ANCRUM NEW PARISH CHURCH.

LORD, the memorial-stone we lay
    Of this the house we raise to Thee;
Look down on this auspicious day,
    And let this place a Bethel be!
Here in this house may sinners see
    The ladder rear'd 'twixt earth and heaven —
The Christ who died on Calvary,
    That all our sins might be forgiven.

The heavens contain Thee not, O Lord!
　　Far less may this the house we build;
Yet meanest cot, where Thou'rt ador'd,
　　Is with Shekinah-glory filled.
And here may human souls be thrill'd
　　With glorious lifting views of Thee,
And each wild wave of trouble still'd
　　Into most blest serenity.

O may a table here be spread,
　　To which God's saints shall joyful go;
Here be dispens'd the Living Bread,
　　And here the Living Waters flow!
Here, too, may Eschol's clusters glow—
　　The goodly clusters of the land;
Yea, here may men God's mercy know—
　　God's loving-kindness understand.

Lord, make the earthly fetters start,
　　The strong man's goods despoil Thou here;
With godly grief here touch the heart,
　　Bid flow the penitential tear.
And here, with rapturous vision clear,
　　Of sins through Thee absolv'd, forgiven,
Remove Thou every guilty fear,
　　And lift the soul from earth to heaven.

A spiritual birthplace make it, Lord;
　　May thousands at the last declare
That they were thro' Thy quickening Word
　　Begotten in this house of prayer.

May young and old here truly share
   God's own provision, free and full ;
And here be plenty, and to spare,
   For every mercy-seeking soul.

God's grace for aye be here the theme !
   God's grace reveal'd by Thee, whose blood
At Calvary flow'd, a cleansing stream
   To reconcile us unto God.
O Thou who bor'st the accursed load !
   Who vanquish'd all our mighty foes !
Make in the preacher's heart abode,
   That he may here God's grace disclose ;

That he may here with boldness speak
   Of Thee, the Church's risen Head—
The Prince of Peace, the Saviour meek,
   Who stood up in a lost world's stead ;
The First-Begotten from the dead—
   He who victorious o'er the grave
Captivity in fetters led,
   And glorious gifts to rebels gave.

Yes, let Thy servant here proclaim,
   As Thou dost bid him in Thy Word,
A free salvation thro' Thy name—
   Thy mighty name, O blessed Lord !
Thus shall the blessing forth be pour'd,
   And sinners cease from God to roam ;
While saints shall joy with one accord
   To see Thy glorious kingdom come.

ON LEAVING ANCRUM AND ALEWATER.

ADIEU, a long, a fond adieu
    To Ancrum and Alewater;
Dear Border homes and scenes so fair,
And granddames, grandsires, parents there,
    And many a son and daughter!

How much conspir'd, dear village-scene,
    In my esteem to raise thee!
Thy loveliness, thine old-time charm,
Thy wealth of friendly feeling warm,
    Ah, still for these I'll praise thee!

Yea, in thy silent moments oft
    I'll think with deep emotion
Of friends belov'd I found in thee,
Friends who must have where'er I be
    My soul's unfeign'd devotion.

And, Ale, thy splendid Eden-scenes
    I still must fondly cherish;
Yea, memory methinks must fail
Before thy charming scenes, O Ale,
    Within me pale or perish.

Flow on, sweet stream, to Teviot flow!
    By bank and scaur meander!
'Mong sweeter, lovelier scenes than thine,
'Mong charms that more delightful shine,
    I scarcely hope to wander.

How fair thy haughs, thy banks and scaurs,
  When Spring goes forward sowing
Her gems with liberal hand o'er earth,
When oaks fresh golden leaves put forth,
  And hawthorns white are blowing !

And lovely they when all array'd
  In Summer's glorious fulness ;
But lovelier still when deep through all
Red Autumn breathes, and sere leaves fall
  Through Nature's Sabbath stillness.

Yes, flow, sweet stream, to Teviot flow !
  In fancy now returning
For one brief moment unto thee,
More of thy loveliness I see,
  Far more thereof I'm learning.

How good the sight of yon old mill !
  How sweet its situation
Within thine opening vale so fair !
How beautiful it seemeth there
  In its lone sequestration !

And those old Coventanter-caves,
  I fain would tell their story :
I fain would picture in my rhymes
The noble hearts of olden times
  Who lend thee still a glory.

E.

And yonder is the ancient kirk
    Amid God's Acre standing!
How good it was therein to be—
And now it seems to speak to me
    Even with a voice commanding.

" Pilgrim of Time!" it seems to say,
    " Beware thou of confiding
Too much in pleasant things below:
Like shadows here men come and go,
    Yea, here there's no abiding.

" Put thou thy confidence in God,
    And reckon thou His favour
More than this earthly scene can give;
Yea, that thou to His glory live
    Unceasingly endeavour!

" Valiant for Heaven's eternal truth,
    Press on to worlds more glorious;
On till thy battle-day shall close,
On till o'er all thy mighty foes
    Through Christ thou prove victorious!"

But there, too, is the old-time bridge,
    The bridge like shoe of maiden,
Which graceful spans, O Ale, thy stream—
I see it as in waking dream,
    Dear Fancy's light array'd in.

Ah, oft I've cross'd that lovely bridge,
   And by yon dairy wended ;
And climbing up the steepy slope,
Like one still warm with youthful hope,
   The Castle Hill ascended.

And o'er yon bold wild Castle Hill,
   Through boulders, whins, and brackens,
In fancy now I onward stray,
And, while I wonted scenes survey,
   Great joy within me wakens.

Again I look on Ancrum Moor,
   And feel such inspiration
Of high exploits men there did do
As well might fire a lover true
   Of our old Scottish nation.

Yea, on I go until I come
   To where Maid Lilyard's lying ;
And pausing there, I proud peruse
Her epitaph so bold, and muse
   On her heroic dying.

Her lover slain, her country wrong'd,
   Some say that these impell'd her
To mix in Ancrum's bloody fight ;
Wherein, 'tis sure, she fought with might
   As long as might upheld her.

Her lover slain, her country wrong'd—
   Yes, these, I trow, uniting
Into one potent cause, did urge
The maid into red battle's surge,
   Where fell she nobly fighting.

Rest on, O sacred dust, rest on,
   Far in your woodland temple !
Maid Lilyard is a memory now,
Yet she has left, we must allow,
   A heroine's example.

But now a long, a fond adieu
   To Ancrum and Alewater ;
Dear Border homes and scenes so fair,
And granddames, grandsires, parents there,
   And many a son and daughter !

PART II

Nature-Sketches and other Poems.

STRAY LEAVES FROM THE BOOK OF SPRING.

'Tis Spring! triumphant on her way
  She hies o'er hills and plains;
Yea, in the golden car of day
  She rides through city lanes.
The pale mechanic starts to see
A rich unwonted brilliancy
  Glimpsing athwart his dingy room,
And, as the hart for water-brooks,
He pants for glens and flow'ry nooks,
  And for the rathe primroses' exquisite heartsome bloom.

Morn, glorious morn, with high triumphal song,
And jewell'd grass, and leafing trees, and scents,
And visitations infinitely rich
Of the world's morning left so far behind!
At such a time might angels walk the earth.
No tiniest leaf is stirring in the woods.
All, all is still, except the tuneful birds.
These now keep up a heavenly interchange
Of call and answer. Higher, ever higher,
Swells and ascends the rapturous symphony,

Until the tremulous palpitating air
Rings with a holy yet delirious joy !
Now let me wander forth beside this stream,
Which, hermit-like, betakes itself beneath
Hazelly banks ; yet sparkles soon again
In the glad day : then soon again is hid,
Its presence in no wise conjecturable,
Save by the vivid greenness of its marge ;
Then, finally, its haunts obscure all past,
Yonder appears in gushing liberty,
The slenderest thread of lovely burnished gold.
An exquisite symbol of a human life,
Humble and true, most surely is this stream.
Ah, many a tree and plant and flower are blest
By its unfailing liberal ministry.

O what a joy 'tis now to wander forth
Thro' Nature's lovely Spring-transfigur'd scenes !
'Tis Spring ! what heart of babe, or boy, or man,
Leaps not to meet the glory-bringing Spring ?
Oh, heart-affecting those first messages,
Her snowdrops and her crocuses, which she sends
To winter-wearied men !   How rich, how rare
Her preparations, and when she has spread
Her banquet, who, oh who that tastes thereof
Is not as happy as a marriage guest ?
'Tis Spring ! and yet how lately did we hear
Grim ruffian Winter strike his forest harp,
And summon all his grisly warriors forth.
How late we heard the tempest's furious drums
Sounding among the hills, and saw the snows
Swirling one wild tumultuous mountainous sea !

Where were ye then, ye blythesome choristers?
Ah! in deep shades and coverts ye were hid,
And silent, shivering pass'd the boreal day.
And ye, poor timid sheep, how did ye 'scape
A snowy sepulture?   Ah! safe in stells
And bieldy plantins ye were timely hous'd
By careful shepherd, whose quick, practis'd eye
Had seen in the grim cloud the brewing storm!
How chang'd the scene!   The birds in vernal tents
Are at high festival.   Hark! hark! they sing.
'Tis Spring! 'tis Spring!   The lambkins on the lea,
And he who tends them—the blythe shepherd boy—
Confess 'tis Spring!   The myriad-arrow'd sun,
Transpiercing the dew-beaded corn; all sights
And impulses abroad declare 'tis Spring!
O come, my toil-worn brother, come away,
And taste her banquet in the primrose dells;
Come, mount with me the shining, misty hills,
And catch the rapturous shimmer of her face!

Of all the pretty sights of vernal days,
Oh, prettiest this—lambkins on the green meads
Vieing with one another in the race—
Some choosing aged oak, some daisied knoll,
Some bush of furze, or moss-clad stump for goal.
Pleasant 'tis, too, to see the husbandman
Driving his cattle—heifers and strong steers—
From winter sheds to yet untasted fields.
Bellowing for joy o'er new-found liberty,
The herd rush on, shrill barkers at their heels,
And sturdy urchins, brandishing rude staves,
Following officious, but most bent on sport.

How rich in glee is boy-life on a farm !
Each season to the rustic younker brings
Anticipated joy.   His joy unfolds
With the unfolding year, on till he sees
His sturdy sire mow down the golden grain ;
Or till with kindred hearts, with merry playmates,
He gathers nuts low down in hazel dell.
Nor doth grim Winter chill it :—glad at morn
He sees the window-panes all scribbled o'er
With strange handwriting, or with goblin shapes
Cramm'd full—Jack Frost's miraculous handiwork !
Ah ! then rare expectation takes his heart ;
Sly o'er the threshold steps he, and beholds
Long gleaming ice-dirks hanging from the eaves,
And all before him ice-bound pools, and hills
Grizzled like eld ; and, boisterously glad,
He girds himself for winter's hardy sports.
For him the village school does much, and much
Parental training ; but what Nature does
Is all her own.   Ranging her free domains
His limbs acquire elastic strength, his mind
An indestructible ingenuousness,
And, as his receptivity may be,
Bright store of images, rich seed of thought.

Now o'er the muirs the curlew clamours shrill,
And lapwings pipe their intermittent strains,
Wheeling and diving in eccentric flights.
The corncrake harsh—as yet but seldom heard—
From village crofter's green-hain'd patch strikes in,
Steadily chanting his laborious song.
And, hark ! the cuckoo blithely lifts her voice

O'er the high woods !   The aged forester,
Bent at his task, now hears, as in a dream,
The quavering call, and o'er his gleaming axe
Pauses, while struggling memory brings back
His boyhood's image.   Now he thinks how he,
A satchell'd schoolboy, conning morning tasks
In the rural way, would start to hear that voice,
And peer and peer again throughout the wood,
If peradventure he some form might see.

But see yon children of humility
That take the lowest place and highest soar,
And, soaring, sing with heavenliest melody—
See yon gay larks bounding from heathy beds
To greet day's king, or bathe their pinions grey
In the calm golden fountains of the morn !
Up ! up ! they mount ! cleaving the exquisite air
With valiant wing ; nor pause, save when they shout
"Excelsior !" till their aërial heights
They have attain'd.   There, long and rapt they sing,
Making the solitary places glad.

It is a city holiday ; a sweet
And rich spring day.   In parti-colour'd throngs
Glad families from the city hasten forth
Into the country round.   O, ye green fields,
Ye rural lanes, ye woods, but ye'll delight
Some hearts to-day : your fresh, your heavenly charm
Most sweetly will insert itself into
Some toilsome lives to-day, restorative balm
Ye now will shed on many a weary soul.

O, now to mark the joy of human faces,
The joy of men, of women, and of children,
Hastening into the kind embrace of Nature!
See yon poor family! not long they've left
Their dingy home in city alley dark,
To taste the spring, to spend one blessed day
With birds, and trees, and flowers, and all fair things
Wherewith the Lord His world has richly stor'd.
See, now they've sighted Nature's fair domains—
Vales, woods, fields, swelling hills before them stretch
In fine perspective.   'Tis a glorious sight,
A sight of glamour and enchantment sweet
To one and all.   The happy children run
Ahead of the fond parents, who, with looks,
True love-looks, follow them.   The two dear boys,
Poor tiny men, o'erbrim with ecstasy;
For now they've near'd the woods, and now they hear
The ringing songs of mavises and merles,
The cooings tender of soft cushat doves,
And the caw-cawings of great sooty crows,
All going on together.   Joyful concert!
But passing strange!   And see the daughters three,
Small children-women, the eldest having a care
Of her two weaker sisters; see where they,
Intent on beauty that delights the eye,
Are busy—oh, how busy!—gathering
Bright flowers for nosegays to adorn their home.
O happy day, for parents and for children!
Day that will be remember'd 'mong the days;
Day that will, star-like, shine from out the past.
How oft they'll think of it, and dream of it,
And wish for others of the like to come!

Ah! if 'tis sad that Nature's fair domains
Should by a single soul be unenjoyed,
How mournful is the thought of human crowds
Who, pent in cities, never once have seen
The untarnish'd face of Nature!   Human crowds
Who never once have known the glorious joy
Which warbling woods, fresh fields, and breezy hills,
And vales with clear meandering streams inspire!
What! was not man at first form'd from the soil,
And given the largest property in the soil?
What! was not earth made fully his at first?
Was not the universe arrang'd, adorn'd
For him—God's topmost work? Had he not space,
Clear elbow-room at first: room to enlarge,
And right to all the broadening influences,
The sanctities, and sweet moralities
Of Nature's scenes?   O why, then, has all this
Been cruelly forgot? or, what is worse,
Persistently ignor'd?   Why in this earth,
This birthright of each member of the race,
Have countless thousands neither part nor lot,
So far as right to till and to enjoy
Some little portion of the same's concern'd?
O why these crowds congested in the dark
Of cities and of towns? these crowds so sunk,
So terribly defaced by crime and woe,
And the mere savage struggle for bare life?
Has earth no spaces left untill'd and void,
Where the poor stranded members of the race—
The miserable, the sinning—might begin
Their life anew; yea, make salubrious homes,
And find the joy of hope in fruitful toil?

Work on, ye brave philanthropists! work on!
The day is dawning.   Men are rising up
Here, there, and everywhere to care for man.
The unutterable sin of callousness
And self-indulgence now is being expos'd.
The long-continued, cruel sacrifice
Of millions for a few more striking grows.
Work on! a grand theocracy the world
Shall yet present; a blessed government,
Where man to man in links indissoluble
Of brotherhood shall be joined; where God in Christ
Shall be the reigning soul and crown of all.

Cities and towns with justice often boast
Of ancient glory.   Often they can show
Structures impressive, finely eloquent,
Of a rich, antique time; fair Gothic piles
That tell how pious and how gifted were
Our ancient sires; ay, and that plainly say
That in them rul'd the heavenly harmonies.
Yet, after all, such noble piles are only
Works of men's hands.   Nature is God's own work,
And has a glory and antiquity
Surpassing all that to men's work belongs.
And Nature's ever old, yet ever young!
'Tis true she has her frosty winter sleep,
When youth seems dead and gone; but soon again
She wakes and smiles—soon bravely says again,
I have the spirit of eternal youth!
'Tis wonderful! 'tis passing wonderful!
What generations of our sires have look'd
Upon these hills and these irriguous vales,

And seen them nothing other than they're now;
These powerful features of this mighty world
Remain essentially the same so long!

Yes, Nature venerable, glorious,
Nature remains essentially the same
Thro' the long ages.   Calmly she beholds
The mystery of human life go on;
The generations crowding in the rear
Of generations; and the ceaseless march
Of human beings to the final goal.
Calmly she sees all this; and why should we
Be stunn'd or burden'd with the thought of it?
Albeit the life of man must needs be short,
Thank God! it may be made heroical,
And fruitful of perennial bright results!
Yes, every noble thought, or word, or deed
Given to the world, both blesses the giver of it
And swells and strengthens the nobility
By which the world's maintain'd and held from wreck.
No, brother, 'tis not lost! not lost, my sister!
Thy contribution to the good and true,
Small though it may seem, lives on eternally.
'Tis true it may have seem'd like tiny rill
That has diffus'd itself 'mong thankless soils,
Or that has been absorb'd by arid sands:
'Tis true that it may now elude thy ken,
And seem like what has been but now is not;
Yet be assur'd of this, that it lives on
Somewhere and somewise in God's universe.
No, nothing good can e'er be lost or die!
How could it?   Every good thing kindred is

With God Himself.   Oh, let us then take heart,
And use our hours and powers as best we can !
Dauntless, invincible, let us go on,
Sure as the Godlike in us here is found ;
Sure as we've worthy hopes and aspirations,
Shooting strong-wing'd beyond the empyrean ;
Sure as we've struggles towards ideals high—
Yea, inward strainings like to throes of birth—
And sure as these are not a mockery ;
Sure as we justly, too, may look to find
Somewhere, if not on earth, the due reward
Of struggles and of sufferings bravely borne
For truth and right—so sure there is a life
Higher and fuller waiting on the brave !

'Tis unto noble souls, to spirits true,
That Nature doth reveal her inmost heart ;
For they alone have sympathy with Him
Who is at once her Author and her Soul.
A tacit covenant with such she makes ;
Becomes their stanch ally, their teacher true ;
And reinforcements brings their better minds.
Further and further leads she them into
Her holy of holies.   But the brutish man
She doth repudiate and quite disclaim.
Her forms of purity and exquisite grace
Each day reprove him, and by contrast show
His vast deformity and loathsomeness.
Nor is she only 'gainst the brutish man,
But 'gainst the sordid ; 'gainst the petty-soul'd ;
'Gainst false and slothful natures ; yea, 'gainst all
Who are disloyal to her God and King.

The sordid? Yes, in her great liberal style,
In her fine generous fashion, Nature shows
A true contempt of sordid-mindedness.
Of splendid wealth, of various goodliness,
How lavish she; with what effusion gives!
The petty-soul'd? Nay, large-soul'd Nature shows
To such no favour. Magnanimity,
Candour, and loving-kindness, she supports,
And quite abhors all little-mindedness.
The false? O name them not! no part have they
In greatly truthful Nature. Loyally
She runs her cycles; works her great results
With sterling rectitude and honesty.
Nor have the slothful part or lot with her.
She still unresting and unhasting moves,
Achieving and effecting gloriously,
Upon the lines whereon Omnipotence
Hath set her going! But the slothful man
To Heaven, to man, and to himself is false:
A wretched cumberer of the ground is he;
Nor physical, nor spiritual health is his.
His inner self is like a stagnant pool,
It sours and rots. The insect in the breeze,
Laboriously fulfilling its small part,
Might look on him with pitying contempt!

Thee, work, I praise; for thou dost merit praise.
O stern entail on all the human race
Since e'er the Lord the primal curse pronounc'd;
Yet wondrous blessing in God's wondrous plan,
Without which mind and body cannot thrive
Or be develop'd into manly prime:

Thou art God's medicine for ten thousand ills;
Ten thousand baleful poisons canst subdue.
Thou grand condition on which we attain
Life's blessings with their flavour unimpair'd,
Fresh and innocuous; there's hope for him
Who unto thee right honestly conforms:
That man will rise; yea, who will bounds prescribe
Unto his manifold prosperity?
Yes, blessed he who, while God gives him strength,
Will work right honestly.   What better fate
To mortal man can fall than that he fill
His life's allotted years with honest work?
Oh, Labour hath her aristocracy,
Her men of large and generous sympathies;
Her men whose lives are true—none are so true—
Unto Creation's plan.   And who that sees
Such in their virtue's strenuous exercise,
Their honesty, their manly dignity,
But will declare they are the finest sight
Upon God's earth?   Yes, rather far would I
Be one of such—even one who earns his bread
By honest toil, and sleeps an honest sleep,
Even the tir'd labourer's innocent well-earn'd sleep,
Than the most splendid idler 'neath the sun.

But cease my desultory strain!   'Tis now
The afternoon, and I have roam'd about
Since early morn, having no other food
Than spiritual sustenance.   Yes, cease my strain;
Some new Spring-day may waken thee again.

TO THE SKYLARK.

O MINSTREL sweet, that lead'st the choir
  Of the gay vernal morning;
Now while thou wak'st thy muirland lyre,
  Thou seraph-like art burning;
  And still thou art uprising,
  The solitude surprising
With the wild joyance of thy love-taught lay:
  O herald of spring gladness,
  Thou speak'st of ended sadness,
Hymning the birth of the new vernal day.

Now thou dost take with minstrel grace
  Thy high aërial station:
Sweet bird! well dost thou fill thy place
  Within God's fair creation.
  Now at heaven's portal singing,
  Thou, far and wide, art flinging
A dancing show'r of bright courageous song:
  O thing of hope and glory,
  Though rough the way before me,
I'll think of thee, and bid my heart be strong.

'Tis done! Now thou dost drop, sweet bird,
  Down from thy height of beauty;
May my best blessing now reward
  Thee for thy minstrel duty!
  Now 'mong the blooming heather,
  Thou and thy mate together,

F

Will one brief precious hour of rapture spend :
   Oh, may I be as thou art,
   A happy, brave, and true heart,
And dwell so low, so sing, and so ascend !

AN AUTUMN SONG.

I LOVE, I love to ecstasy
   The lovely Autumn days,
When the hills and vales and cornfields lie
So charmedly, so placidly,
   In a golden mystic haze.

O to see the reapers at their toil,
   And the stooks in even rows !
O to see the harvest treasures rich,
And to pluck the Autumn fruitage which
   By the country highways grows !

And O the beauteous Autumn nights,
   When the glorious moon comes forth,
When solemn red, like a huge flame-shield,
Or some face where burning love's reveal'd,
   She's lying o'er the earth !

O it's still to rove, it's still to dream
   In the flaming lunar light :
It's away 'mong the stooks of golden grain,
It's away o'er the mountain and the plain,
   In the mystic Autumn night !

My God ! but the earth is beautiful !
    It is all so fair to see !
And Thee would I praise, and Thee would I bless
For the glory and the loveliness
    That the Autumn brings to me.

A DREAM OF YOUTH.

"Gieb meine Jugend mir zurück."—*Goethe.*

I DREAM'D that my lost youth I found,
    And that my heart again
Replied, with many a joyous bound,
    To Hope's wild thrilling strain.
Again with lightsome step and free
I wander'd o'er the jewell'd lea,
    Brushing the pearly dew ;
Again with youth's clear eyes look'd forth
Upon a variegated earth
    All living and all new.

I mark'd where morning's glowing kiss
    Gladden'd the fair green hills ;
I mark'd her smile of perfect bliss
    Beam in the crystal rills ;
I watch'd the day advancing pour
Thro' Nature all her splendid store,
    Till every secret glen,
Each nook, each crevice small was fill'd,
And impulses of rapture thrill'd
    Thro' birds and beasts and men.

Now, even 'neath age's heaviness
    Had life a gladness been;
But life with youth implied a bliss,
    Like a fount-upspringing sheen;
And I was young, O I was young,
A living soul, but late upsprung
    God's glorious world to see;
To marvel at the wondrous sight,
And to draw in its subtle light,
    Its love, its mystery!

Now from her dwelling at my feet
    The lark did merrily spring,
Up and still up she sped to greet
    The day's majestic king;
Again, as news from heaven, I heard
The music of the aspiring bird,
    Again I strained my sight,
Till on the pinnacle of day
I mark'd her pouring forth her lay,
    A cherub of delight.

O joy to hear the minstrel lark,
    When on us lies life's dew!
O joy great Nature's charms to mark
    When life is fresh and new!
My bliss it rose, it mounted up,
Until methought my being's cup
    Could nothing more contain;
My heart went forth in melody—
In rhythmic numbers bold and free
    Fast flowed the impassion'd strain.

Again I sang, right nobly sang
   The songs which genius loves ;
And sweet the hills and valleys rang,
   Rang sweet the listening groves.
The cherub-singer poised on high
Had not a sweeter strain than I,
   Or one more eloquent ;
For youth's glad thoughts were all mine own,
And Fancy from her mystic throne
   To me kind greetings sent.

But soon the splendid day gave place
   To pensive, holy night,
And the mild moon with queenly grace
   Dispens'd a silvery light.
And now 'mid Nature's calm I stood
Within a lone and ancient wood
   With one long lov'd, long sought ;
Her face intent was turn'd to mine—
Her face so human and divine,
   So full of earnest thought.

My life's young love !   Could it again
   In very truth be she
Who in the ancient forest fane
   Now kept her tryst with me ?
Yes, it was she, and O how fair,
How calm, how bright, how free from care,
   How modest, kind, and good !
Just in her wonted simple dress,
Just in the tender loveliness
   Of early maidenhood !

I thought that she again to me
    Did give her promise true;
And that the heavens look'd down to see
    Two hearts their vows renew.
Again I took her to my heart,
Again I vow'd we ne'er would part,
    But 'neath one roof-tree dwell;
Again her cheek to mine she laid,
While in low, serious tones she said:
    "Dear love, I love thee well!"

"I love thee well, ah yes," she said,
    "Thou hast my whole heart won;
And I life's path with thee will tread
    Till the sands of life are run;
I'll be thy bride, thy happy bride,
And aye will I be at thy side
    With help and succour kind;
In weal and woe, till death us part,
Thou in this leal and faithful heart
    Thy comfort true wilt find."

But soon methought our tryst was o'er
    Within the moonlit wood,
And day again had risen to pour
    O'er earth her golden flood.
It was our marriage-day; and we
Now midst a nuptial company
    Stood in a chamber small,
While the thrice-holy rite was done
That join'd our lives and made us one
    To steer right on thro' all!

Such was my dream!—too soon 'twas flown;
  Too soon again I knew
That she I lov'd was long, long gone,
  And youth long vanished too.
Too soon I knew I'd dream'd, yet O,
Yonder where flowers immortal blow,
  And life's river aye runs clear,
My love! my youth! ye're waiting there,
More radiant than what time ye were
  My bright possession here!

WHEN THE SPRING FLINGS HER GEMS.

WHEN the Spring flings her gems over mountain and lea,
  And Nature is jewell'd and rob'd like a bride,
Wilt thou go, wilt thou go to the woodlands with me,
  Thro' the fair forest dells wilt thou walk at my side?
In the fair forest dells, when the oak leaves are new,
  And when sweet is the scent of the evergreen pine,
Thou with Nature's fine joy wilt be thrill'd thro' and thro',
  And this heart still will beat in glad concert with thine.

In fellowship sweet, thro' the woodlands we'll rove,
  And beauty we'll meet in each lovely wood way;
We will list to the wild birds discoursing of love,
  To each fair primrose nook we'll delightedly stray.
Like children, we'll revel 'mong gems of the Spring,
  And thro' the blue day sweet our converse will be;
And not till the gloaming spreads o'er us her wing,
  Not till then, not till then I'll turn homeward with thee.

NIGHT AND NATURE.

'Tis profitable for mortal man to walk
In deep retiréd thought through Nature's scenes
What time red autumn through the forest fane
Sheds dim cathedral light, or glory meek,
Like that of suffering saint; or when the spring
Exhaleth balm throughout the wakening earth.
And if he the night season should affect,
'Tis profitable more! Lo! now the night
Comes pacing on to starry harmonies.
Softly, oh softly, with dew-sandall'd feet,
She steals upon us, a serene high presence.
See, where the moon, ascending, looketh down
As if she were earth's tutelary angel.
'Tis the same moon the patriarchs look'd upon,
Which Joshua made stand still in Ajalon's vale.
All through earth's stormy fortunes, through these acts
Of earth's long tragedy, has she, handmaid-like,
Waited upon her in deep loyalty.
And see, the starry host comes peering forth
Like diamonds of first water! Seem they not
Like lights to guide us to our Father's house?
Perhaps, one avenue of luminaries,
They light the way to God's own palace-gates.

How fair this vernal night! This wild green glen
Is all a richly-garnish'd, holy place.
Sweet now the air with glen and woodland scents,
Which the soft dews set free. Nature is lapp'd

In a luxurious calm—a calm most sweet,
Yet as the hush of worlds.   Yon snowy thorn,
So motionless, stooping o'er the steep, resembles
Some white-hair'd sire bent in devotion deep.
Only the rippling burn gives audible voice,
While, like a silver thread, fantastically
It twists among green banks !   Silence and beauty
O'er all things brood ; yea, like twin-goddesses,
Enthron'd on yonder dark star-silver'd peaks,
They awful sit.   The flocks rest on the sward ;
The birds repose in deep embowering shades.
Peace seems the inalienable heritage
Of every tenant of the field and brake.

Oh for a harp wherewith I now might voice
Great Nature in her high beatitude ;
A harp, withal, wherewith I might uplift
To high beatitude the souls of men !
Why, why are we so little apt to rise
To sacred altitudes ?   Why so backslidden
From the divine and fair, that mighty Nature,
Even in her loftiest moods, can little move us ?
Why grow we narrow, mean, and mammonite ;
The slaves of selfishness, the dwarfs of men ?
Why join we us unto the race of fools,
With whom the question of all questions still
Is—how much sweetness each for self can suck
Out of the world's enormous honeycomb ?
What ! have the ages toil'd for us in vain ?
Shall we, to whom they have transmitted on
Such glorious wealth, such cumulative good,
Not know what we are heirs of, and transmit

Our rich inheritance, with fair increase,
Onward to future times, to future men?
Up, up, my brother! wherefore should we cumber
The world with barrenness, or further fool it
With unreality?   For real men,
For men belonging to humanity,
Men mission'd to meet man's deep necessity,
The world still cries.   'Tis time that we reach up
Unto the summit of our manly build;
Time that we throw away the spurious thing,
And clear ourselves from folly; time that we
Be men of justice and of manly love;
Time that we do our utmost for the world,
Nor, Cain-like, say, "Am I my brother's keeper?"
Time that we be with Heaven co-operating,
And helping in Truth's kingdom bright and fair.

Why should we grasp at what must prove our bane?
We were not born to grovel here, enslav'd
In mammon's mine; nor yet to toil and strive
For place or power, as if our life lay there.
We were not born to aim at world-renown,
As if no life were glorious without this.
We were not born for pleasure, nor should we say,
"Let us eat and drink, for to-morrow we shall die."
But we were born for this sublimest end,
To live the truth—through wisdom strong within
God's pure effulgent image to express.
Voices of patriarchs, prophets, and apostles,
And martyrs (chief, of Christ the great God-martyr);
Voices of all the God-like, dead and living,
Call us to take our place at God's free banquet,

And, on the strength of what we there may eat,
To live for truth and for humanity.
'Tis he, and he alone. that lives the truth
That truly comprehends the beautiful;
Kingly is he without a diadem,
And priestly without imposition of hands;
For God hath made him king and priest, and he
Doth walk erect; doth move confederate
With what is God-like round him; yea, the earth
Is unto him the very Temple Courts
Of the Most High.   At morn he goes to toil,
And God goes with him.   He returns at eve,
And God is with him.   His whole life is prayer,
A ceaseless intercession for the race.

OCTOBER.

Hail, ye lowne days of October—
  Golden-girdled autumn days!
Hail, ye groves, august and sober!
  Hail, ye pensive leaf-strown ways!

Sunk are now the groves in sadness,
  Save what time the feather'd throng,
Rous'd by sunshine into gladness, .
  Pour an intermittent song.

True, it happens in the valley,
  Even when fall dull drizzling showers,
That one hears birds singing gaily,
  Like brave souls when fortune lowers.

'Tis a time for solemn musing :
  Now, in meditative mood,
Nature's ample page perusing,
  Let me roam through field and wood.

Through the dim glades let me wander,
  Where lone-murmuring flows the rill;
'Mid this pensive autumn grandeur
  Let me pause upon the hill.

Mighty Nature ! in all ages
  Man from thee high Truth has learn'd,
And both babes and hoary sages
  Have in thee a friend discern'd.

Now thy sacred influence stealing,
  Like deep music, o'er my heart,
Wakens in me thought and feeling,
  Strengthens all my better part.

A STORY ABOUT HIGHLAND PREACHINGS.

O, HAPPY season of boyhood ! when like some most
    glorious poem
Life opens out upon us ; when on all things the shimmer of
    newness
Rests like a beautiful charm ; when Hope, like a guardian
    angel,
Leads us onward through regions of Paradisiacal beauty ;
When, with elastic step, we walk the flower-sprinkled
    valleys,

And climb, with free breath, the hills, and survey the
    smiling landscape
With a delightful sense of unconfin'd possession.
O time, when simplicity reigns, and when we dream of no
    evil;
When the rose is without a thorn, and each human heart is
    noble,
Or when at least we credit it with an untarnished nobility.
O time, when imagination is glowing with a fervour
Like that of the sun; that man, though a millionaire, I'll
    not envy,
Who of thee doth not fondly cherish some reminiscences
    golden.

Ah, reminiscences golden have I of the season of boyhood,
And not the least golden are those in connection with old
    Highland preachings
And the famous "Men of the North." Of these worthies
    my father
Might almost be reckoned one. Indeed, I would call him
Equal to any among them in respect to Christian experi-
    ence,
And mental gifts, and equipment of knowledge, and of
    wisdom.
Only in natural fluency was he in a measure inferior.
In truth, 'tis with pride that I think that mine was such a
    father.
A father, whose life was to me the noblest of inspirations;
Who into me breath'd that spirit that wrought within me
    and shap'd me;
Yea, that has shap'd my course in God's world until this
    present.

'Tis thirty years since my father pass'd into God's Sabbath
 eternal,
Yet to-day 'tis still fresh in my mind how, after the day's
 darg,
I, seated with him and my mother beside a glorious peat-
 fire,
Would listen to his accounts of the famous "men" and the
 preachings
Among the wild hills ;—the preachings which would last four
 or five days running.
Him, I, a youngster, hearing, would earnestly wish he'd soon
 take me
To one of those wonderful gatherings ; but always the place
 of assembly
Was so remote, that it was not till my fifteenth year was
 opening
That the privilege I enjoy'd ; and then I alone did travel,
Or with not a creature excepting brave Donald, our Highland pony.

Let me tell how it came about: My father and I were
 working,
Industriously doing our best at the close of our usual peat
 season
In a bog not far from our house ; and Donald, our pony,
 just mentioned,
Was standing quite near on a knoll. My father, while
 forward plodding,
Forgot not his favourite topic. His talk, however, to-day,
 while
Of preachings in general, had reference to a particular series
Of services " to take place," as he said, " not so very far off

On an estate call'd Valdalloch." Ah, well I remember
    asking
"How far did he think?" and hearing him answer "nigh
    forty miles distant."
Whereupon (I remember, too) I threw a long look at
    Donald,
And, before I well knew what I did, my plan was formed
    and expounded.
"Father," I cried, "if you'll give me our Donald, and a
    half-sovereign
To meet my sundry expenses, I'll venture to go to the
    preachings."
A heroical project most surely, even with sagacious good
    Donald !
The ferries, glen, corries, woods, moorlands between me
    and wish'd-for Valdalloch,
For my inexperience in travel might prove all too much ; yet
    my father
Admir'd my boldness, and plainly construed it as some-
    thing right manlike.
Discouragement none he urg'd ; he just put me off by
    saying,
" We'll see by and by about it ; for me, my dear son, all
    too clearly
The farm must hinder me going: I cannot, I must not now
    leave it."
Thus stay'd the matter a week—a week we anent it were
    silent ;
Yet my plan, though hastily form'd was held by ; and now
    I was oftener
Patting Donald's neck ; and to him I spoke of it some-
    times,

If to no one else : such, I say, for a week was the posture
    of matters.
But rest had I none till my scheme was brought a second
    time forward,
And this time my father chim'd in, consenting to all that
    was in it :
Donald and the half-sovereign, and whatever else might be
    fitting,
Were to be mine.   I, a boy, seem'd to pass at a bound into
    manhood.

Tuesday it was when my father consented.   I was to be
    ready
Against the following Monday — auspicious day ! — for
    departure.   '
Two days' journey, 'twas thought, would bring me to
    Valdalloch:
And since Friday was fixed for the first of the series of
    services,
I would probably have to spend the Wednesday and the
    Thursday,
As well as the nights and somewhat more of the days of the
    preachings,
At the mansion of Valdalloch.   Which to do I e'en was
    right willing,
For Mr. Campbell M'Lean, the master there, and the
    owner
Of the Valdalloch estate, was my father's friend of long
    standing,
And would entertain me gladly.   To him then wrote my
    father,
Announcing my intention, and asking him to expect me.

And now my mother was busy with needles and with
    scissors
Producing for me a new jacket, and I. reliev'd from farm-
    labours,
Was getting sundry repairs effected on saddle and bridle
At the neighbouring clachan. To this just add that I was
    making
Donald's further acquaintance, and you will see my picture
In these preparation days. But why should I now linger
On the threshold of events? Why speak of my father's
    instructions
Regarding the route? The day — a day as brilliantly
    shining
As e'er illumin'd the hills—it arrived, it looked in at our
    windows.

In the usual course of things, heavily I slept; yea, most
    mornings
Needed to be " knock'd up." This morning, before my
    parents
Were cognizant of aught here, I was up and had donn'd
    my trousers.
I shall never forget how I shouted, to my parents' rude
    awakening,
When from the right trousers' pocket a shining half-
    sovereign
I drew, and from the left three shillings and a sixpence,
And what an infinitude seem'd of pennies and of halfpennies.
Of a truth the good brownies had been at work in the
    weird time of midnight.
But here, too, was the jacket my mother had sat up to
    finish ;

A jacket surpassing the best that I had yet gone to church in!
And here was a bonnet, a beauty, a glengarry, which surely
    my mother
Had secretly bought 'gainst this moment. No wonder my
    boyish gladness
So wildly, so madly o'erflowed. But soon I sat down to a
    breakfast
Verily fit for a king: and having to this done full justice,
And just when my kind good mother was plying me with
    entreaties
To eat still more, lo! my father, who to Donald's wants
    had attended,
Appear'd with him at the door. And now the due farewell
    expressions
Having been interchanged, I on the bridle-reins seizing,
Put foot in stirrup, and vaulted lightly into the saddle:
And, the prompting word being given, my Donald he bore
    me forward
At a rattling trot. O the eyes of my father and my mother,
They were fix'd on me till the moment that, by a sudden
    turning
Of the road, I was hid 'mong the hills! Then, reining in
    my Donald,
I bade him pursue his way in a tranquil spirit of leisure.
The fresh mountain breeze had sprung up, and blew in my
    face, and a gladness
Of a breezy exultant kind in my heart was now upwelling.

And now for my glad recollections of my journey to
    Valdalloch.
Three ferries the first day we cross'd, but Donald always
    behav'd him

In the most beautiful manner possible for a Highland pony.
Towards night we came to an inn where I accommodation
And refreshments obtain'd, and which, behind it, afforded
    stabling
And hay for Donald. The bill, which on Thursday morning
    I settled,
Was exactly one shilling and twopence. Indeed, the good
    old landlord
Would have let me off scot-free, but my pride refus'd to
    allow it.

The second day of my journey was one of glorious
    brightness
Both as to things without and things within my spirit;
But our goal we saw not that day, nor indeed for some time
    after:
We'd doubtless wander'd, yet nought of care or anxiety
    knew I.
By picturesque glen, craggy hill, and pretty homely shieling
We onward went right glad. The way I sometimes asked
    for
When a shepherd lad I met, or a kindly mountain maiden;
Sometimes vied with the lark, of the way or aught else
    oblivious:
Sometimes, too, I'd dismount and walk by my equine
    companion;
And more than once I rested by a wimplin' burn. I
    remember
Even wading a burn, and gumping the silver trout, while
    Donald
Grazed on a green haugh-patch; and trouts indeed in great
    plenty

I got, and soon arriving at a wayside shieling, I found them
Enough to regale myself, and a family, too, of young
    children.

'Twas on this second day of our journey we came to a forest,
A great and lonesome forest which, alas ! we could not steer
    clear off,
Thro' which our way did lie.   No; I cannot express the
    feelings
Of dread that shot thro' my soul, causing the perspiration
To stand like beads on my face, while now we went
    sounding, sounding
Along a perilous way ; along even the most sepulchral
And terror-haunted of paths. Poor Donald, he, too, was taken
By the cold distemper of fear. Most plainly I saw him shiver,
But soon, by dint of hard cheering, I had him into a gallop,
At which he kept on for two hours, or a space little short
    of that period,
Till, poet's licence to use, this levianthan forest disgor'd us
Into the light of day, and into the gayest oasis.
'Twas about mid-afternoon, and the place was so perfectly
    charming
After the gruesome forest, that I was almost persuaded
To grant to my equine friend and myself some pause as
    reward for
Our bravery and toils.   But, thinking again of the matter,
I bade my trusty companion pace slowly through the fair
    landscape,
Resolving, instead, we should spend the night at the first
    house that offer'd
Refreshment and rest, be it inn, or only some rush-cover'd
    shieling.

'Twas a shieling to which we soon came, even the humble
    abode of a shepherd.

An elderly dame of a grave and most hospitable appearance

Show'd face—even the shepherd's wife, the mistress of the
    dwelling.

She my story learning, did ask me in manner most friendly

To spend at her cottage the night ; and at the same moment
    she pointed

To a byre at hand where my pony could find accommoda.
    tion.

A stall next a Highland crummie's soon lodged my equine
    companion.

There a supply of the sweetest of mountain hay having
    given him,

I return'd to the house, where the mistress receiv'd me with
    hearty gladness.

Anon the shepherd came home from the moor, and me he
    greeted

After a kindly sort, and the frankest conversation

Was set agoing between us. This, during the plenteous
    supper

Which the goodwife set before us ; yea, on till bed time
    lasted.

The happiest remembrance is mine of this most worthy
    couple.

O muse, just one thing record ! nay, do not call it a trifle !

Taking off my boots for the night, I found to my grief that
    the uppers

Of one of them had been torn (without doubt in my wild
    forest-gallop) ;

And while the rent beholding in rather a lachrymose
    manner,

I felt that the man and his wife were looking and condoling.

But nothing was said, not a syllable. How mighty, then, was
my wonder,

Next morn when I woke, to find that the boot that I had
griev'd for

Was there with its fellow beside my bed as right as if St.
Crispin

Himself might have done it. With joy that scarcely can
even be imagin'd

I drew them on and was shod, yea, splendidly shod, for my
journey.

As for my host and hostess, somehow their manner this
morning

Warded off talking, yea, seem'd to say, we'd rather not
have it,

At least not about the boot, that affair unto you so
momentous !

Once indeed I ventur'd a remark thereanent of the briefest,

But no response it evok'd. Ah, well, I knew that the
shepherd

Had either been cobbler himself, or had been to some son
of St. Crispin

The while that I slept. Ah me ! this kindness still looks
wondrous charming !

Breakfast and worship soon over, again I was mounted on
Donald,

And forward, forward, forward, was faring to Valdalloch.

'Twas the third of my journeying days—even so ! yet my
goal still seem'd distant.

Perhaps I was misdirected ; perhaps there were two
Valdallochs.

Ah, little or nothing it matter'd; no end was there found of
  good people;
Even "all along the line" me such from afar were hailing,
As if they'd been parents, and brothers, and sisters, and
  other relations;
And dreaming of prospects ahead I still kept cheering my
  spirit.
Indeed, it appears I had lapsed just a little too far into
  dreamland.
One thing was growing full plain—my way was becoming a
  puzzle,
Nor knew I at all where to turn. Three, four, five, or six
  ways meeting,
Or coming quite near together, became for my choice equal
  claimants.
'Twas a strange confusion all: the world for me was
  becoming
Amazingly like a maze: 'mid "perplexing paths" many
Was I now, and minus a clue the slightest, the feeblest, to
  guide me.
What now could I do but commend me to Him whom my
  parents had taught me
To look to, and having so done, let Donald go as he
  listed.
Even so I did. To my Guide and Guardian unseen looking
  wholly,
The reins I on Donald's neck loosely laid and encourag'd
  him forward.
Even thus, as one blind, was I led in a way that I knew
  not;
Thus in paths I had not known was I most certainly
  guided.

And soon I perceiv'd in the distance a luminous, cloudy
    appearance.
Smoke slantwise pierc'd, as by myriads of brilliantly clear
    solar lances,
It seem'd, and soon I was sure this smoke was the peat-reek
    familiar
Arising from houses along an open hillside extending.
I was approaching a clachan.   Now thro' its luminous
    envelope
It took shape, it grew into form.   'Twas a picture glowing,
    romantic.
Donald now prick'd up his ears, and pac'd in a livelier
    fashion.
On stabling and sweet mountain hay his thoughts were most
    plainly directed ;
And objection I had none that he should enjoy these
    blessings
As soon as they could be reach'd.   I, too, with intensity
    long'd for
A hospital board and intercourse loving and cheerful
With the social race of men.   My Donald's objects and
    mine, then,
In nowise collided.   "Go forward," I cried, "O my quad-
    ruped trusty ;
Stabling full soon thou shalt have, and no end of most
    pleasant refreshment."
Thus did I cheer him on, till, before very long, we were
    going
Up what I'd call the main street of the town had the place
    not consisted
Of this street and no more.   This street, then, we now were
    gladly ascending,

Donald briskly walking, I confidently allowing
The reins to hang loose on his neck.   O, how could I dream
    for a moment
That he was going to make an escapade wholly disgraceful ?

A baker's shop we were passing—a shop in the course of
    getting
Adorn'd with a cream-colour'd paint.   A painter lad on the
    outside ;
Another within—these were busy plying at it with dexterous
    brushes :
And while the olfactory nerves of a quadruped stricken with
    hunger
Might the presence of bread or meals recognise, I of this
    am certain
That mortal was none could be sure of ought but the odour
    of paint-pots.
That Donald, however, perceiv'd a glorious savour of some-
    thing
Was shortly made most plain.   On passing the shop, without
    warning
One wild, wild leap he made ; or leaps, it might be a
    series
He shopward made.   I, by instinct, then duck'd down my
    head for a mercy !
Yes, 'twas a mercy I did so, for he the shop had invaded,
Leaping in without regard to painters, or paint-pots, or
    counter,
Or the baker and his wife, who behind the counter were
    standing.
The counter he simply knock'd down ; and how in the
    world I manag'd

To escape without broken limbs, or, in spite of my ducking
    down timely,
Without a fractur'd cranium (for the door was low and
    narrow,
As if it had been achiev'd in some quaint, old monkish
    era)
It baffles me to conceive.   I only know that the baker
And the baker's wife in an instant from Donald's back had
    me lifted;
And that the painter lads, in a stern and ferocious manner,
Laid hands on my four-footed friend, who went away with
    them somewhat
"As an ox to the slaughter goes, or a fool to the stocks'
    correction."
And well might he thus go away, for a madder, foolhardier
    action
Never Highland pony did.   As for me, in the strangest
    position
I found myself—in the hands of the baker and his help-
    meet.
So suddenly there I had come, and was such an egregious
    object—
Paint, paint, creamy paint all over! that I fairly cried out
    in my sorrow,
"Donald, O Donald, thou fool; yea, thou totally foolish
    descendant
Of fools! for surely nought else were thy fathers and
    mothers,
That was too, too bad!"   In such terms I cried, but the
    baker and helpmeet
Both sooth'd me, and began rubbing my clothes in a style
    energetic;

And by rubbing for two stricken hours (nearly all which
    time the painters
Were scouring away at Donald) the paint disappear'd, but
    the odour,
The smell persistent remaining!   O, how could I go to the
    preachings;
Ay, how? and again I broke down, and again the good
    couple 'gan soothing,
And what with kind words, and dinner and tea, I was com-
    forted fully;
And when pressed to remain overnight, I yielded with
    pleasure,
And the more so, since Donald, the traitor, could also be
    car'd for.

So over the night I stay'd with this hospitable couple,
And next morning was on the road pursu'd by their good
    wishes.
'Twas Thursday—fourth day of my journey; a circuitous
    way had I travell'd,
But now was correctly inform'd that Valdalloch was all but
    accomplish'd.
I could laugh at my rambles now, and even at Donald's
    mad frolic;
Though of that I must bear yet awhile an odorous re-
    minder.
And laugh I did, and encourag'd him; and soon I could
    see we were coming
Into a country still finer than that through which I'd been
    passing.
But not long had I to study the look of the country around
    me,

For soon to a wall, high and massive, good Donald was
    bearing me forward ;
And my road, soon I saw, ran along 'neath the shade of
    this wall ; yea, it rounded
The wall at a place where 'twas form'd in a sort of semicircle.
Pushing on, anon I came to a garden gate where I, halting,
Saw the jessamin'd front of a quaint and lovely old mansion.
Five seconds I there was not station'd when I saw the front
    door open,
And a gentleman, tall and well-dress'd, appeared, and just
    like an arrow
Shot down the garden walk to the gate where I was standing.
"Are you Johnny M'Leod?" cried he, in accents anxiously
    quavering ;
And having own'd to my name—"O, my bairn ! my dear
    bairn !" said he, wailing,
"Say where have ye been ? Ochon ! sure we for you have
    been looking
For two days at least." O, reader, you may guess that I
    was puzzled
By these greetings, sudden and strange. Ah, yes, it was
    rather perplexing,
Till on me it softly dawn'd that this was the friend of my
    father,
Mr. Campbell M·Lean ; and this, too, the house of
    Valdalloch.

What words may ever make known all that's meant by a
    true Highland welcome ;
Even such a welcome as now I received into the stately
And well-appointed mansion of my father's friend ? To his
    lady,

Mrs. Campbell M'Lean, I was introduced first; then in
    order
To each of the guests, and of these there were many, both
    men and women,
In view of the glorious days, in view of the services
    sacred.
Mrs. Campbell M'Lean was kindness itself; she embrac'd
    me,
Imprinting a kiss on my cheek; and the guests her
    example follow'd.
With effusion it all was done, yet with the most perfect
    decorum.
Ah, surely in Highland hearts there's a poetry wholly
    surpassing!
And with these folk I'd to stay, and attend the services
    sacred;
And Donald was in clover, and I could enjoy the wisdom
Of the wondrous " men of the North," and, perhaps, the
    more wondrous women.

Space here forbids a description of these so famous worthies.
In the main they were surely most lovely and talented-
    looking figures—
The woman of great faith pre-eminent stood 'mong the
    women;
Her, the pious, the stately, I cannot o'erlook in justice.
A majesty and a beauty undoubtedly were about her,
Such as in any company had made her an object of notice;
And I've heard that such was her energy that she would
    come to a village,
And would visit some thirty houses therein, in every house
    bestowing

Advice and counsel, and all betwixt the morning and
　　evening.
A story about her as follows used once to be widely
　　current :
In view of services such as those we now were awaiting,
Staying was she at a Highland manse, where Doctor
　　M'Donald—
Yclept " the Apostle "—and many another fam'd worthy
　　was gather'd.
Near to the manse, and o'erlook'd by one or two of its
　　windows,
Was an immemorial churchyard, whereinto arrivals of
　　people
Now constantly dropp'd, there to wait the hour of the open-
　　air preachings.
The woman of great faith now mark'd from a window these
　　people,
And by and by seeing them sitting or leaning upon the
　　tombstones,
Apparently hungry and faint after long and tiresome
　　journeys,
Began to cast about how she might do them a kindness.
The manse folk had not yet din'd, for as yet 'twas but
　　barely noonday,
So the larder as yet was full of cold prepar'd provisions.
The woman of great faith form'd, therefore, her plan without
　　trouble,
And being a woman incisive, her plan was soon bodied in
　　action.
With the calmness imperturbable of an unwavering assurance,
And in next to no time she'd got the larder supplies into
　　towels

And out at a back door, and in 'mong the folk in the
    churchyard ;
And soon were these supplies laid out on some table-like
    tombstones
Before the hungry people, who in a twinkling despatch'd
    them.
Ah ! one may imagine, more easily than tell, the peculiar
    feelings
With which the guests in the manse, just when they were
    seated for dinner
(For the thing only then got wind), receiv'd the most
    marvellous announcement
Of the minister's housekeeper old—to wit, that the stores
    of the larder
Whereon she had reckon'd had vanished in quite a mysteri-
    ous manner ;
And that they must dine to-day, if to-day they'd have ought
    for the body,
On bread and cheese, and eggs, and a cup of warm tea or
    coffee.

Just one more word regarding this justly famous woman :
A new-married pair had resolv'd, that if God should give
    them a daughter,
They would give her the name of the woman for whom
    they had most veneration—
The woman of great faith ; and the more so since she, the
    resplendent,
Had none of kin to transmit her name to the new genera-
    tions.
How great, then, the joy of the pair when a daughter was
    given them,

And when they upon her bestow'd the name so belov'd and
    so honour'd
But if their joy was great, not less, but far greater, their sorrow
When the little one died. But soon another daughter was
    given them,
And to this, too, they gave the name. But, O darksome
    dispensation !
This one an imbecile turn'd, most awfully thus revealing
(Even so the parents read it) that Heaven had never
    intended
The name of the saintly one to be thus handed onward :
That her record was on high, and nothing else was needed.

But the preachings ! O fain would I speak concerning
    those wonderful preachings
Which in the following days took place in the glen of
    Valdalloch ;
Fain would I tell of the crowds of solemn-faced worshipping
    people,
And the grand old Psalms of David far away 'mong the
    mountains rolling ;
Fain would I sing of those scenes whence springs old
    Scotia's grandeur,
And 'tis with reluctance I check my desire for further
    writing.

Just one thing, and I have done—a trifle, yet here I
    record it :
One of the " Men," Duncan Bane, was a huge and inveterate
    snuffer—
Religious, talented, eloquent, was he even on all hands
    admitted ;

Yet I, for one, deeply felt that his never-ending snuffing
Pull'd down his tone, and enfeebled even much of his real
religion.
I therefore took it upon me with gentleness to advise him.
Yes, young though I was, so I did, and Duncan heard me
with patience.
"Ay, lad," said he, "what you say is all very good, very
zealous;
But my 'mill' has so long been a comfort, I cannot now
discard it."
The day after that of our talk, alack! Duncan Bane lost the
comfort
Whereof he did speak. His "mill" was no more in his
large waistcoat pocket.
Now I admit that it was not in the least surprising that
Duncan
At this juncture thought I had taken it in surreptitious
manner,
To the end I might wile him away from a nasty, useless
habit;
But that he should go forth (and this was just his procedure),
Spreading the rash report that I, John M'Leod, had
stolen it,
This must always appear to me a matter inscrutable.
Three days he went about seeking the "mill" and spreading
Industriously this report; but me, it seem'd, he avoided.
I could not tell what it meant; but at last I could bear it
no longer.
I sought him, I found him, I told him that it pain'd me to
hear he was spreading
A report against me, and bade him think better of what he
was doing.

H

Then quoting a passage of Scripture, I show'd what concerns us concerns, too,

The benignant Powers above; "and though the matter," I
argued,

" Be but that thing called a snuff-box, yet at least if the loss
thereof causes

Dispeace, it may not unfitly be made a subject of prayer."

To this the good man agreed, and own'd he'd been wrong
in rushing

To unwarrantable conclusions, and forthwith we bow'd
together

In prayer.   After which I suggested that perhaps he had
dropped the snuff-mill

At a certain place on a hill where I knew that he and others

Had gone aside for talk and cheerful Christian communion.

But Duncan thought it unlikely he in such a place would
find it ;

"Yet," said he, " I'll go and I'll search, although I do
nothing

But please my dear bairn."   He went, he found the thing
that he sought for.

Never shall I forget that moment he came to me showing

The unconscious cause of annoyance, the thing he had lost
and recover'd

After meikle pain.   Then he flung his long arms about me,

Kiss'd me and hugg'd me fondly; confess'd with tears his
error

In putting upon me guilt of which I had been guiltless.

Then, thanking me for the advice I had taken it on me to
give him—

To wit, to give up the " mill "—he remark'd that babes were
oft wiser

Than full-grown men; but added that now of years he'd
    seen eighty,
And he trow'd it was scarcely worth while that he should
    take the trouble
To renounce the thing he'd enjoy'd for half-a-century fully,
And especially since, after all, 'twas to him a precious
    comfort.

So much for my memories golden connected with old
    Highland Preachings

SCOTLAND'S WOODS.

OF Scotland's proud hills let our bards sing the praises,
    Or hymn Scotland's streams as they ripple along
Through glens of wild brackens and meadows of daisies,
    But methinks Scotland's woods are as worthy of song.
See, see where the cottage and mansion they're shading;
    Where they slide from the plain down the valley so deep;
Where they nod o'er the scaur; where they're valiantly
    spreading
    Away, high away o'er the wild hilly steep.

Yes, see where they spread high away grandly towering;
    Birks, hazels, oaks, rowans, planes, beeches, and pines!
See, see! shedding joy o'er the sward sweetly flowering,
    The sun through the fine sylvan tracery shines!
Ah, the woods—how delightful they are when they're closing
    Around us their fresh lovely garments of green!
And for wand'ring, or musing, or placid reposing,
    Where, where is the place like the fair woodland scene?

O it's up in the woods when the spring there is storing
  Her myrrh and frankincense in plant and in flower;
When the songsters their sweet nuptial anthems are pouring;
  When the cushat strikes in with a soft soothing power!
It's there when the oak in its new dress is glowing;
  When the charming wood-vistas are flooded with light;
When the rowans and hawthorns are gloriously blowing:
  It is there I would joy in glad Nature's delight.

Yes, it's up in the woods when the summer is tender;
  When the freshness, the bloom, and the song is yet new;
O it's up 'mong the gladness, the beauty, the splendour,
  While life is still opening in pure virgin dew.
And it's there when the year's ampler banquet is ready;
  When the blaeberry bonny the youngster can please;
When the foxglove stands high on the crag like a lady,
  And rings her rich bells in the soft passing breeze.

O it's up in the woods in the fine August weather
  I'd forget for a little this world's anxious pain;
It is there I'd adorn me with sprig o' the heather,
  And dream o'er the dreams of life's morning again!
And I'd list to the bee, where, nigh drowsy with pleasure,
  In quest of the honey through heath blooms she roves;
And my Fancy would also go gather her treasure—
  The rich mental treasure that poesy loves.

And it's up in the woods for a glorious ramble,
  When a rich autumn haze over Nature is spread;
When black, luscious black, are the berries of bramble,
  And the rowans, the hips, and the haws blushing red.

And when the wan leaves are all falling and falling,
   'Mid the Sabbath o' Nature so sacred, so fine,
Let me rove in the woodlands recalling, recalling
   The loves and the friends o' the days o' langsyne.

Yea, it's up in the woods when the grim desolations
   Of winter is there in its dreariness seen ;
When the trees stand up bare like great skeleton nations,
   O it's there, too, I'd be in the frost-air so keen.
'Mong the snaw-pouther'd wrecks o' the year I would
     wander ;
   I would pause, look around on the stern winter scene ;
I would take it a' in, and withal I would ponder
   What the winter that waits on us mortals may mean.

JEAN LINDSAY AND HER CALLANT.

A HOMELY INCIDENT TURNED INTO SCOTTISH VERSE.

AFAR 'mong Kirkcudbright's wild heathery mountains,
'Mong her mosses and muirlands, her lochs and her fountains,
Jean Lindsay did dwell, wi' wee Hughie, her callant,
And 'bout these I now mean to indite a bit ballant.

Their housie was wee, and wi' rashes was theekit ;
A bit wusp held thegither its chimla, peat-reekit ;
And its twa bits o' winnocks were ilk a wee wicket,
And its east wa' was green wi' a fine ivy thicket.

And the peat-stack did stand at the wast wa' weel bieldit,
While a yaird 'fore the door bonnie tata craps yieldit,
And through the yaird hedge aft wad bore Hugh's wee
     lammie,
While owre it wad look Jean's braw Galloway crummie.

At the back of the house Jean had twa grumpies feeding,
And a cock ye might see his seraglio leading
Aftentimes to the stye; and at hand was a gutter
Where fat ducks, a full score, through the hale day wad
     squatter.

Frae what I hae mentioned thus far in my ballant,
Gey routhie, ye'll see, were auld Jean and her callant;
But now for a tale whilk I fain wad be telling
About this fine pair in their cantie bit dwelling.

Lo! the broad day is shining, and to their peat-casting
Jean and Hugh doon the gate should hae lang syne been
     hasting;
But still they're no steerin'—O Jean, honest woman,
What, what can it mean? 'tis a thing quite uncommon.

O Jean, thy braw tryst wi' thy neebours has fa'en through;
At three in the morning the glens they were gaun through
To meet thee, to help thee to do thy peat-casting;
O Jean, whatna time wi' thy sloth thou art wasting!

Get up, thoughtless woman! wi' shame I am burning,
The casters will sune frae their darg be returning;
Lo! the day's mounted high, and the noon is approaching;
The broad sun will its zenith be speedily touching.

O Jean, what has happened? Strange things I am fearing;
I'm sure it is serious, or ye wad be steering;
Perhaps thou and Hughie wi' peat-reek are smeekit;
Perhaps cauld in death ye by this time are streekit.

But, hush! I'm by nature owre much gi'en to fearing;
Hark! hark! the dear inmates at last they are steering!
See! see! Heaven be praised! the bit door is flung open,
And the auld-fashion'd pair owre the door-step are loupin'.

"My certies," cried Jean, "I've a while been a woman,
But I trow I hae never ken'd aught sae uncommon."
She look'd roun'—ilka winnock wi' brackens was stappit!
She look'd up—lo! the lum-tap wi' divots was happit!

The brackens she pu'd frae the winnocks fu' speedy,
And Hughie, he cleared the lum-tap unco ready;
Whilk done, they astonied their dwelling re-enter,
And for the fine ferlie some reasons now venture.

O, now they think this thing, and that, and the ither,
And aften they pit a' their reasons thegither,
And choose frae them a', but 'tis only confusion,
And the ferlie still waits on its proper solution.

Douce Jean, though she neither had learning nor riches,
Could hardly believe or in warlocks or witches;
Yet seemed a' her neebours sae sober and cannie,
The deed she could faither nor mither on any.

But after some thinking—for Jean she was gleg aye—
She thocht o' a fair-spoken hizzie ca'd Peggie;
E'en bonnie Peg Gibson, sae slee and sae cannie—
Yes, yes! she was liker the prankie than any.

Yet this, deep within her, Jean meantime did bury,
And sent Hughie aff to the moss in a hurry;
O then cam' her neebours, and they, without swither,
Mainteen'd it was Peg, and it was na anither.

When her neebours had gane, and while Jean was just
    thinkin'
O' what she had heard, wha should step in like winkin'
But slee Peggie Gibson?—wha thus began sayin':
"Oh, I'm sorry, dear Jean, that this morning ye lay in!"

"O yes!" broke in Jean, "I had ettled to waken
Just when in the east the bricht day should be breakin',
And to hie wi' my laddie away without wasting
E'en a moment o' time to a big day's peat-casting.

"And, in truth, as to wak'ning I was na a sluggard,
But the dawn was to me as a wearifu' laggard;
O lang, lang dark hours was I wide awake lying,
O lang, lang was I for the bricht dawning sighing.

"I thocht 'twad turn licht, so I lay hardly winkin';
And for hours upon end I was thinkin' and thinkin',
On this thing and that thing, on blythe things and sad
    things,
Till lif seem'd a lott'ry o' guid things and bad things.

"And aye 'mid my thochts did I think o' my casting,
Afraid I a moment o' time should be wasting;
But still, when I look'd for a ray in my chaumer,
The midnight I felt, wi' its darkness and glaumer.

" I haena a clock, as ye ken, my dear Peggie,
But when the dawn breaks, I may say, I am gleg aye;
But now I was puzzled, for still in my chaumer
The midnight I felt, wi' its darkness and glamour.

" But at last I, impatient and sair, and e'en dreadin'
That some strange mirky judgment owre a' might be
        spreading,
Sprang up, cried on Hugh, and the door quick flung open,
Swith my laddie and I owre the doorstep were loupin'.

" 'Twas day, 'twas braid day, the bright sun had arisen,
And I look'd about, daz'd like ane out some dark prison;
I look'd roun'—ilka winnock wi' brackens was stappit!
I look'd up—lo! the lum-tap wi' divots was happit!"

Now Peg, who had listen'd to a' this narration,
Said, "Jean! how I grieve owre thy heavy vexation;
But wha, wha could do thing sae black and uncommon?"
"O, they say," spak' Jean Lindsay, "'twas thee, Peggie,
        woman!"

MARY-ANNIE

THOU hast gone awa' frae me,
        Mary-Annie;
And thy face nae mair I'll see,
        Mary-Annie;
It is hidden out o' sight,
And extinguish'd is the light
That made the dull day bright,
        Mary-Annie.

Thou wert "baith guid and fair,"
　　　Mary-Annie;
Thou wert blythe and debonair,
　　　Mary-Annie;
Ane wha never knew a fear;
Making holy music here;
Like a well upspringing clear,
　　　Mary-Annie.

Was thy going gain to thee,
　　　Mary-Annie?
Oh, the loss it was to me,
　　　Mary-Annie!
'Twas a mighty, mighty blow;
'Twas a swelling, swelling woe;
And no further grief could go,
　　　Mary-Annie.

Now the winter tempests sing,
　　　Mary-Annie;
Nature languishes for spring,
　　　Mary-Annie;
And the spring will come again
And renew the hill and plain,
But I'll wander a' my lane,
　　　Mary-Annie.

Nae mair among green hills,
　　　Mary-Annie,
We'll track the shining rills,
　　　Mary-Annie;

Nae mair the earth will seem,
In its glory and its gleam,
Half a fact and half a dream,
  Mary-Annie.

There's a light beheld no more,
  Mary-Annie;
There's a loss we must deplore,
  Mary-Annie;
There's a wound that's slow to heal,
There's the absence o' the leal,
Wha aye sought our chiefest weal,
  Mary-Annie.

A MOTHER'S LAMENT IN WINTER.

Now Boreas fierce, on icy wing,
 Sweeps o'er the hills with wild career:
The dark storm-spirit seems to sing,
 And make harsh music in mine ear.

Yet blow, thou bitter Boreas, blow!
 Yet sing, thou dark storm-spirit, sing!
Now, since my joy is buried low,
 A solace sweet to me ye bring.

Dark spirit, sing! rude Boreas, blow!
 Lament with me for Nature's child!
Oh, I must now full lonely go,
 A pilgrim through a dreary wild.

And is he gone, the lov'd, the true;
  He who was gude as he was fair;
He, the sweet blossom that I knew
  At once as Heaven's and Nature's heir?

I had but him—the sweetest thing
  That ever blest a woman's e'e;
And he unto my breast did hing,
  And he was a' the warld to me.

I had but him—my boy so true
  Amid a world of grief and wrang;
A sweeter flower it never grew,
  A sweeter bird it never sang.

I had but him—nae mair was given,
  And I was mair than full content;
I little thought that he, by Heaven,
  Was only for a moment lent.

I had but him—oh, now, I miss
  His big blue eyes' brave sunny gleam,
And his small life, all woven of bliss,
  From top to bottom without seam.

Oh, why against my darling boy,
  Fell Death, didst thou launch forth thy dart?
Why didst thou kill the bud of joy
  That nestled sweetly to my heart?

It's O my rose, my white, white rose,
  I miss thy scent and beauty rare;
There's nothing now my spirit knows
  On earth sae winsome and sae fair.

It's O my bird, my bonnie bird,
    That sang sae sweet when days grew dull;
Since last thy tender song I heard
    My heart has been with sadness full.

My last bright hope of bliss below
    Wert thou, dear Nature's chosen child:
Now I must lonely, lonely go,
    A pilgrim through the dreary wild.

NITHSIDE.

YES, there are scenes on earth which memory makes
Like heaven's own gates; lov'd scenes whose mention
    wakes
Within us feelings of such sacredness,
Such power, as human words may ne'er express;
Lov'd scenes to which bright spirits have said farewell,
But left thereon a strange, a subtle spell—
A spell like smile angelic blent with tears,
Which makes them radiant all our coming years!
Such scenes there are; and O, belov'd Nithside,
Thou scene to which methinks some angel-guide
Brought me at first, thou surely art to me
Even one of such. O still, dear place, I see
Thee bath'd in some such tender mystic haze,
As one might see on brightest autumn days.
Still, still I'm borne on Fancy's pinions fleet
To the familiar house and garden sweet;

Still down each lovely flower-edg'd walk I muse;
Pause, look around, the accustom'd scene peruse;
Find it all beauteous-sad, all sacred-fair;
All eloquent of those who once were there!

Ah! sacred scene, so long a cool retreat,
Whereto I from the burden and the heat
Of life's arena came; and, coming, breath'd
That peace which Christ unto His own bequeath'd.
Can I forget or wholly lose that joy,
The noblest, freest, from the world's alloy,
That bliss of friendship which in thee I knew
'Mong hearts whose every throb to mine was true;
'Mong souls the best which mortals here may find
For help, for solace to the immortal mind?
Can I forget those welcomes, warm and free,
Which to the last thy master gave to me;
Yea, how these welcomes would be quite out-done
By my best friend, that master's generous son,
Who made me still with him co-heir of all
Of good or fair that to his lot did fall?

Nithside! how charming in those days thou wert!
Yet that which drew and knit to thee my heart
Was the dear presence of thine inmates lov'd,
Those two who still to heavenly measures mov'd,
That sire, that son!—That sire! O could I paint
That well-belovèd venerable saint,
Then on my page methinks would be portrayed
An old man after Heaven's own pattern made:
A man of fine impressive form and face,
Of ancient dignity, of courtliest grace;

A man with soul deep in Heaven's love baptiz'd,
A beauteous Gaius of the Church of Christ.
That son! ah, could I paint him, then I ween
The faithfullest of sons would here be seen :
A son such as old age might well desire ;
Yea, one well worthy of the noblest sire ;
A son obedient, pious, courteous, brave,
As noble sire for help and stay could have.

Yes, charming scene, 'twas still those splendid two
Who with thy crowning charm did thee endue ;
'Twas they who made thee fair exceedingly,
The loveliest house of hospitality,
Regalement, hope, to which 'twas e'er my lot,
By seen or unseen angel, to be brought!
Twas they who made thee to us journeyers here
A place midway unto a happier sphere ;
A place to which tir'd wanderers might draw nigh,
And find earth's food and God's refreshments high ;
A place of fruitful palms and crystal springs ;
A place still fann'd by holy angel wings !—
Yes, he who once beheld that sire and son,
As like twin lights in thee, Nithside, they shone,
He who in thee beheld them, bore from thee
The treasure of a sacred memory ;
Something to lighten many a cloudy day ;
Something to cheer him forward on life's way.

Ah, might they have remained—have still been found
Going from year to year their usual round !
Might'st thou, so long their lovely Eden scene,
Still, still to them a dwelling-place have been !

Might'st thou have claim'd them still!   Yet that dear sire
Saw many things in this our world transpire;
Saw nigh an hundred years, then sweetly fell
Upon that rest that is unspeakable.
His latest words—" Pray without ceasing!" brought
Strength to his son wherewith to bear his lot—
And strength he needed much; for soon 'twas plain
That he in thee no longer could remain.
Heaven's call, "Go hence!" full soon 'twas his to hear;
And soon he girt him for another sphere:
From thee he went, ah, never to return,
Howe'er for thee his heart might sorely yearn.

THE ORPHAN MAID.

I saw her first when o'er her hung
The day's triumphal glories young;
    When hope full on her smiled;
When in her home she flourish'd bright
In her admiring parents' sight,
    Their darling, only child.

And then I own'd that she was fair—
In brilliant curls her flaxen hair
    Unto her waist hung down;
And hers was sure no common face,
And form of more symmetric grace
    Ne'er wore a rustic gown.

She seem'd indeed like graceful fawn,
And round her shone the richest dawn;
    Yet me she did not move:
A something needed yet the maid,
A certain soft pathetic shade,
    To wake within me love.

But when I found her out again,
She then had suffer'd grief and pain;
    Her parents both were laid
In the cold grave, and her dear home
Grief's sanctuary had become
    To her, poor orphan maid.

'Twas then she did my feelings stir;
'Twas then I long'd, beholding her,
    To be her dearest friend;
Her friend beyond all friends, that I
Might still devotedly be nigh
    To shield her to life's end.

Ah, no! I have not skill to tell,
Even if you urg'd, how it befell
    That we so quickly saw
All in each other—let me say
That each was drawn to each that day
    By some mysterious law.

Her words at first were few; yet I
Quick felt the sorrow of her eye
    And of her drooping head:

I

Ah, well I knew what it did mean,
And O I thought I'd never seen
        A fairer, sadder maid.

Her words, I say, at first were few
But, as the leal and friendly do,
        At home she did me make
And as I'd come from far, her board
She spread with what she could afford,
        And I thereof did take.

Refresh'd ere long with her good cheer,
Unto the lovely maiden dear
        I undivided turn'd ;
And of the changes in her home,
And heavy sorrows lately come
        On her young life, I learn'd.

I listen'd unto all she said ;
I heard the lovely orphan maid,
        And marked her bursting grief :
And, oh ! I thought, " If true man's love
Can aid her, surely mine will prove
        To her a true relief."

And soon, yea, almost ere I wist,
Love's glorious dayspring I confess'd—
        Confess'd with zeal intense :
But, ah ! no word she said to this—
Only her tear-dew'd loveliness
        Ray'd matchless eloquence,

I waited for her spoken thought,
Until, my eagerness o'erwrought :
    "Be mine!" I cried, "sweet maid ;
Thine orphanhood I'll bless and cheer,
And, oh! thy sky will yet be clear,
    Without one dimming shade !"

I took her hand full tenderly ;
I sought to move her to reply
    To these warm words of mine :
"Such as I am," at length she said,
"Such as I am, an orphan maid,
    Dear youth, I'm wholly thine !'

'Twas done! I clasp'd her to my heart,
And vow'd that we no more would part,
    But be a wedded pair.
"O come," I said, " dear maiden mine,
My kindred will be also thine ;
    Their love we both will share."

Then home in triumph I her led,
And straight I to my parents said,
    "Lo ! here's an orphan maid,
And she's to me more dear than life,
And she is now my promis'd wife ;
    Now with your blessing aid !"

These words I spoke, and many more ;
No need their favour to implore ;
    My parents were her own ;

My sisters were her sisters dear,
And round fraternal hearts sincere
    Her charm at once was thrown.

And soon the auspicious rite was done,
Which, at God's altar, made us one, .
    A husband and a wife;
And, in a home by me prepar'd
For her, the lov'd, full soon we shar'd
    The sweetest cup of life.

And now I see her every day;
And now I often thankful say,
    " Praise God, the fount of good,
Who doth so richly bless our life,
And who has made my lovely wife
    Forget her orphanhood !"

MEMORY'S TREASURES.

KEEP, keep, fond Memory,
    Thy treasures rare !
Which thou hast gleam'd from days
    That knew no care;
Yes, Memory, hoard them well !
For I 'mong them would dwell,
When there's no flower to tell
    Summer was fair.

`Keep thou the records bright
. Of life's young hours,
When sweeter songs of bliss
        Rang thro' the bowers;
When every heart was true,
And the world bright and new,
And in a heavenlier dew
        Open'd the flowers.

Keep the old summers rare,
        Light, scent, and bloom!
And the old harvests rich
        In glow and gloom!
Keep the old hairst-rig's glee
That well'd from hearts so free,
And the warm jollity
        Of harvest home!

Keep the old friends whom love
        Knit in strong bands,
And nights when life's full stream
        Kiss'd flowery strands;
When every heart beat high,
And hope in every eye
Stood eager to descry
        Rich promised lands!

Keep thou the lov'd who have
        These regions cross'd,
Those who now smile on me
        From Heaven's fair coast;

Comrades who died in youth,
Whose souls were sacred truth,
Valour high, melting ruth—
        They are not lost !

Yet, Memory! far above
        All that thou hast,
Keep her who bloom'd within
        The long, long past ;
Bloom'd when by yonder stream,
'Neath the moon's silver beam,
We walk'd as in a dream,
        Dreading no blast.

Keep her bright eyes ; let them
        Still on me shine ;
Keep her truth-speaking face,
        Her dark locks fine ;
Her form so lithe and tall,
Lovely, majestical ;
So shall I fondly call
        Her mine—still mine !

Keep, keep, fond Memory,
        Thy treasures rare !
Which thou hast glean'd from days
        That knew no care ;
Yes, Memory, hoard them well !
For I 'mong them would dwell,
When there's no flower to tell
        Summer was fair.

BARBARA LEE.

'Twas autumn noon, without a breeze,
And slowly, slowly from the trees
The leaves, like golden treasures, fell,
With a motion almost audible;
'Twas then we buried Barbara Lee,
Hard by an ancient churchyard tree;
'Twas then beside her grave I stood,
Long lingering in sorrowing mood.

What feelings of strange loneliness
Did then upon me crowd and press,
Oh, not in dirge, most sad and lone,
Could I make such even feebly known!
Ah! pretty, pretty Barbara Lee,
My life's life seem'd entomb'd with thee;
And nothing in the world was left
Like that of which I was bereft.

Oh, Barbara Lee! that autumn day,
When from thy grave I turn'd away,
I sought some lonely privacy,
Where I, unseen, might weep for thee.
Deep, deep within the faded grove
I mourn'd for thee, my beauteous love,
And for the bright dream-world that fled,
What time I heard that thou wert dead.

Oh, Barbara Lee! oh, Barbara Lee!
I never told my love to thee;
I gaz'd, for most part, from afar
On thee, my young life's radiant star.
Still, still a something seal'd my lips
Till thou hadst pass'd through death's eclipse,
Till it was all too late to tell,
Sweet Barbara, that I lov'd thee well.

Even now, though many a year has pass'd,
Bright maid! since I beheld thee last,
I often think what might have been
Hadst thou not faded from this scene.
I think how, in the moonlight grove,
We might have breath'd our vows of love;
And how, from garish pomp remote,
Bright might have been our common lot.

How sweet wert thou, my village flower!
How rich with only nature's dower!
How rich—yea, how surpassing fair—
Just with a wild rose in thy hair!
Just in thy pretty rustic gown,
Just one of simple nature's own,
Just with thy fresh and glowing heart,
How fair beyond the pomp of art!

I see thee yet, I see thee yet,
Thy locks are like the glossy jet;
Thy blue eyes beam with soul divine;
Thy mouth's a rosebud red and fine;

Thy neck reminds one of the swan;
Thy waist is formed on beauty's plan;
Thy step is rhythmic, bold, and free;
Thou art embodied harmony.

I see thee 'mong the rustic throng,
Dancing the woods and dells among,
Untrammell'd as the rushing rills,
A lovely free child of the hills!
I see thee, gayest of the gay,
Thy life the gladdest summer day:
Ah! what had Death to do with thee,
My pretty, pretty Barbara Lee?

I'M GOING HOME.

I'M going to the low-thatch'd home among the breezy fells;
O'er the heathery moors I'm going to roam, and down the
flowery dells;
I'm going to hear the cuckoo's note and the music of the
rills,
And all the summer voices that float far up 'mong the
verdant hills.

I'm going to the low-thatch'd home which "auld langsyne"
endears,
Which memory in her pictur'd room has kept through
changeful years.
I'll see the porch with roses sweet; I'll ope the well-known
door;
O'er the threshold pass with eager feet, and be at home
once more.

Within the parlour old and brown, which love has sacred
    made,
I'll see the pictures looking down, in a flickering light and
    shade:
From the old walls they'll look on me, as in the years gone
    by,
With a glow of love and loyalty in each fondly sparkling eye.

I'm going to the low-thatch'd home, and happier there I'll be
Than were I 'neath a palace dome of richest masonry;
For the old place it has a spell which nought else has on
    earth,
And can waken thoughts unutterable of the noblest human
    worth.

O there the busy mother dwelt, and things did nobly guide;
And there the priest-like father knelt at morn and eventide;
My brethren, too, you'd find them there, and the happy
    sister-band—
The sister-band as bright and fair as any in the land.

The dear old house, the garden small, the shaded garden
    seat,
For me enchantment hangs o'er all, enchantment heavenly
    sweet:
Yes, happy, happy will I be; and yet, of years long gone,
What memories will awake in me beside yon old hearth-
    stone!

O I will muse by the fire at nights, until my past will
    seem,
In memory's strange chequering lights, like "a dream within
    a dream;"

Yea, then, ah then, within mine ear some voice of ghostly
    tone
Will say, "Poor soul, what dost thou here when all thy
    friends are gone?"

That this will be, full well I know; and yet, whate'er betide,
I to my boyhood's home must go, and there again reside;
O there what yet remains to me of mortal life I'll spend,
And leisurely and thoughtfully attain my latter end.

I'm going to the low-thatch'd home among the breezy fells;
O'er the heathery moors I'm going to roam, and down the
    flowery dells;
I'm going to hear the cuckoo's note and the music of the
    rills,
And all the summer voices that float far up 'mong the
    verdant hills.

OUR AULD GUDEMAN HAS GANE AWA'.

Our hoose he made fu' snug and bricht,
And ilka thing did guide aricht,
While gangin' out and in sae fine,
Frae early morning on till dine.
He keepit a' aboon negleck,
He won for us the warld's respeck,
And naught could daunten us ava,
Till our auld gudeman he gaed awa'.

Alack! it is a waefu' change!
The hoose is eerie noo and strange;
The tic-tac o' the eight-day clock,
Against my heart it seems to knock;

And aft, like bairnie in the dark,
I feel me gaun about my wark ;
And ere I ken, my tears downfa'
For our auld gudeman that's gane awa'.

And oh, in spite o' a' I do,
Things only half are mindit noo ;
Baith folk and things the auld man miss,
And a' about's a wilderness.
The roses that he trained wi' care,
That on the wa' did blume sae fair,
Now dreepin' to the grund they fa',
For our auld gudeman he's gane awa'.

Our stoop has gane ; e'en he wha stude
Unto the last a tower o' gude :
A man o' sense and glorious crack,
Ane nae occasion took aback.
He's gane ! our ae dear stoop is gane ;
We noo life's faucht maun fecht alane ;
Our backs are surely at the wa'
Since our auld gudeman did gang awa'.

Now at the door his dear auld dog
Lies frozen wi' grief unto a log ;
And his pet yowies on the hill
Now shepherdless maun stray at will.
And crummie dauners doon the loan
Like ane wi' sorrow sair fordone ;
And the cocks hae tint their hearty craw
Since our auld gudeman he gaed awa'.

Oh, how will we the winter spend?
What will we do—how will we fend?
Beside the fire yon empty chair,
It says that he'll be back nae mair.
Oh, weary me! joy's fled the hoose
Where we were a' sae bien and croose;
'Tis wae in kitchen and in ha'
Since our auld gudeman he gaed awa'.

THE LOVE O' AULD LANGSYNE.

'Tis now a bonnie summer world
    That glints upon my sight;
And high out ower it is unfurl'd
    Cloud-banners rarely bright.
The landscape, too, has many a charm:
    That's fair, and this is fine;
And here's the dear familiar farm
    We kenn'd sae weel langsyne.

Here are the fields where many a day
    I roam'd to view my sheep,
And where wi' shepherd Will I'd hae
    Discussions strange and deep.
Ah, Will, the man o' doughty tongue,
    Has cross'd life's boundary line;
But he was auld, while she wert young—
    The love o' auld langsyne.

Young, young was she, and her flowing hair
    Had the loveliest jetty shine;
And the blue o' her een might well compare
    Wi' the blue o' the harebell fine.
And she was sweeter than the rose,
    And statelier than the pine;
And in hours o' thought the heart o'erflows
    For the love o' auld langsyne.

And 'tis but right it should, for she
    Ne'er ceas'd to love me weel;
And in every thought she'd think wi' me,
    And in every feeling feel.
And O I never, never heard
    This noble soul repine;
And true was she in every word—
    The love o' auld langsyne.

But here's the house—we're at it now!
    The house with its small plot
Of garden ground; ah, here, I trow,
    Full happy was our lot.
See, round the porch and high out ower
    The roses red still twine;
O ilka thing still speaks wi' power
    Of her I kenn'd langsyne.

'Tis the auld place; I'll ne'er forget
    How she ilk evening came
To meet me at yon rustic yett,
    And bid me welcome hame.

O still come forth, my love, my dear,
 Still star-like on me shine !
Alas ! alas ! she is not here—
 The love o' auld langsyne.

I maunna ask to see the rooms,
 I maunna even stray
Among the lovely garden blooms,
 I'll take this woodland way ;
Yet, O this was her favourite walk !
 My heart I here will tyne !
'Twas here wi' her I wont to talk
 In the days o' auld langsyne.

And yet I fain would walk this wood,
 For the lint white's hame is here,
And the rose, new burstit from the bud,
 Is blooming on the brier.
Here countless charms to me appeal
 To woo this heart of mine ;
I only miss who lov'd me weel—
 The love o' auld langsyne.

But here upon the woodland's skirt,
 Ah, let us pause awhile ;
Here Nature still can thrill the heart
 With rare enchanting smile.
O here, I trow, I could abide
 From morning on till dine,
And muse o'er a' that did betide
 In the days o' auld langsyne.

O, auld langsyne ! O, auld langsyne !
  The words are like a spell,
Recalling more of fair and fine
  Than I can ever tell.
O, auld langsyne ! what days we pass'd
  Among the sheep and kine !
Days all too bright, too fair to last—
  The days o' auld langsyne.

LINES WRITTEN TOWARD THE CLOSE OF A LONG PROTRACTED WINTER.

How doth grim Winter yet prolong his reign !
Hark ! hark ! he strikes and strikes again
His forest harp, re-summoning forth
His grizzly warriors from the North—
Hail, frost, and snow, and yok'd careering winds !
See, see, the poor dim day he blinds
With driving storms ! And see, he binds
The stream upon the precipice !
Behold, 'tis wholly turn'd to ice ;
With icy daggers now the rocky ledges gleam.
The husbandman for the dissolving beam
Now heart-sick longs. Alas ! he must behold
With each new morn a prospect grim and cold ;
Must o'er the tillage-lands, that buried lie
'Neath frozen snows, oft cast an anxious eye ;
Oft cast an anxious eye ; oft wish in vain
For the Spring days and sowing of the grain ;

Must see, too, his late thriving flocks
  All in dumb anguish pine,
And cowering 'neath the tempest's shocks,
  While on poor scentless locks of hay they dine.

Hush, hush, ye winds, or somewhat milder blow!
  Ye snows, withdraw your dazzling, blinding
    folds!
Ah, yonder goes a weary child of woe,
  And a poor babe unto her breast she holds.
Spare her, ye Heavens, and to her prove
Your boundless wealth of pitying love;
And grant that soon some hospitable door
May make her even forget that she is desolate and
    poor!
  But see yon sturdy beggar, stoic wretch,
Fronting the cruel storm with naked breast;
  In kiln and barn, I trow, he's wont to stretch
His limbs, and to compose himself to rest.
Yet doubtless, too, he oft doth find
Both bed and board unto his mind;
And he to-night such cheer may get
  As farm-house kitchen can afford;
Yea, give in sterling coin of wit
  Return for bed and board.
    O heaven-like hospitality,
Ne'er art thou half so fair and blest
As when thou takest to thy breast
    The children of dire want and misery,
And bidd'st them taste the joys of home,
And the extinguished torch of hope relume!

K

Ye favourites of fortune ; ye
Who rest on beds of down ;
Ye who the pinch of poverty
Have never, never known :
Why will ye now, with your full store,
Shut Mercy's bowels up ?
Come, lighten Misery's burdens sore,
And teach Despair to hope !
O why should Prudence, like an icy breath,
Come in as feeling's thrall or feeling's death ?
Ah, never, never can we get from this,
That in the deepest sunk in guilt's abyss
We'll find a being, after all, still human,
One who's our brother-man or sister-woman.
Our brother-man ! Alas ! we do not know
His passions, needs, and miseries wild ;
We do not know what lies within his past :
Perhaps the virus that his life has spoil'd
He drew, a babe, from a wild mother's breast ;
Perhaps misfortune claimed him when a child ;
Hugged him in youth, in manhood held him fast,
And drove him, mad and wretched, on to woe.
Our sister-woman ! Ah, how hard her case
When she, poor flower, is soil'd with dark
disgrace !
How hard ! What ! should we, then, refuse to aid
her
Because it is her sin hath wretched made her ?
Her sin, forsooth ! Let him or her who's none
Make bold to cast at the poor wretch a stone.
Her sin, forsooth ! Nay, let us not begin
To estimate a fellow-creature's sin.

Oh, shame, that frail and erring man
His fellow should presume to scan
     Like an idle gossiper;
Shame that he should profess to see
Or this or that obliquity,
     Or this or that infer;
That he should mount the judge's throne,
Or say to the most worthless one,
     "Stand back! I'm holier!"
And O that ever cruel Mammon
Should mar within our hearts the human,
     Or from our souls efface
The image of the God who made us,
And who refuses not to aid us,
     Whate'er our state or case!
O thou, like nether millstone hard,
  Tyrant to whom poor hirelings bow;
Thou who hast nought of kind regard
  To those less fortunate than thou:
How, how if fortune's wheel should cant,
And land thee in the depths of want,
How would'st thou have it then and in such
    case?
Oh man, dependent on the Eternal's grace,
"Poor pensioner on the bounties of an
    hour,"
Why dost thou arrogate a little power,
  And show a stern, cold face?
Say, what's more lovely, what's more fitting,
Than that we, all but love forgetting,
Unmitigated human still should be
Amid a world so full of care and misery?

But cease, oh cease, my stern appeals,
Man's wretchedness Heaven sees and feels,
    And grief, once full, Heaven 'gins to assuage ;
And Heaven doth make her fountains flow
From earthen vessels, and doth know
    Where to set bounds to Winter's savage rage !
What though grim blustering Winter flout,
    Soon Spring shall break his surly pride,
And soon we'll hear her victor shout
    O'er nature far and wide.
Up, up, poor child of want and sorrow,
Courage again from hope go borrow,
And, oh, from Winter's hardships learn
To prove more wise with Spring's return !
And cheer thee, weary husbandman,
And trust in Providence's plan.
Soon shall kind suns dissolve the snow ;
The golden grain ye soon will sow,
    And soon will rise the tiny verdant spears.
Soon shall you walk through pastures gay,
    And with enraptur'd spirit see
    The ewes and their glad progeny,
Most of them twins, rejoicing in the day !

SPRING AGAIN !

SEE where Spring goes forth repairing
    Every trace of Winter dire ;
Hills, fields, woods, her blessing sharing,
    Don their loveliest attire.

From her long, long sleep awaking,
   Beauty greets us fresh and young,
The deep soul all captive taking
   By her subtle charm and strong.

High above their native heather,
   Larks now shout on valiant wing,
And glad forest hearts together
   Hail the glad and blessed Spring.

Spring again ! O happy moorlands,
   Happy forests, happy glens !
Happy, happy larks and yorlins,
   Finches, mavises, and wrens !

Spring again ! the green's prevailing
   O'er earth's sombre wintry hue,
While in heaven bright clouds are sailing
   O'er the freshest lucid blue.

Spring again ! gay flowers are springing ;
   Streams glide sparkling in the sun ;
Yea, in sweeter cadence singing,
   On they to the ocean run.

Spring again ! yes, here we have her,
   Have her in her loveliest grace ;
Never did we see her braver,
   Or with finer speaking face.

Yes, she's here ; she's here renewing
   This old earth in youth and glee ;
Yea, what things she has been doing
   You on every hand may see.

'Tis the world of old upbuilded
  By the great God-architect;
Yea, 'tis Spring adorn'd and gilded,
  As He did of old direct.

Yes, she's here; her stately going
  Mark I on yon green hillside;
Yea, her shimmering lights are flowing,
  Flowing all through nature wide.

Yes, she's here; she's sweetly speaking
  Home to hearts long winter-chill'd,
Hope and fancy re-awaking
  Their bright airy forms to build.

Yes, she's here with her fine solace,
  Fragrance, bloom, and subtle bliss:
O ye mountains, woods, and valleys,
  Well ye know how sweet she is.

Yes, she's here with all those emblems
  Under which she loves to teach;
This reminder, that resemblance,
  Of high things we fain would reach.

Know'st thou now one feeble creature,
  One who moping sits at home,
Bid him forth 'mid vernal nature,
  Let him feel the Spring has come!

THE LAST SABBATH.

LILY.

Is that the morning sun, Jamie—
    Is that the morning sun?
And has anither Sabbath day
    Upon God's world begun?
Oh, sweet day of the Son of Man!
When kirkward we'd be early gaun;
And do I really see it dawn
    Just when my rest is won, Jamie—
    Just when my rest is won?

JAMIE.

It is the morning sun, Lily—
    It is the morning sun;
Night's weary watches now are past.
    The Sabbath is begun.
The Sabbath is begun, my love,
And dawn now greets thee from above;
By crystal streams full soon thou'lt rove,
    Thy Sabbath never done, Lily—
    Thy Sabbath never done.

LILY.

Thou'lt think o' me when I'm gane, Jamie—
    Thou'lt think o' me when I'm gane;
When 'neath the swaird o' the auld kirkyaird,
    And when thou'rt a' alane?

Thou'lt think o' her wha cheer'd thy past,
Thy flower wha pal'd in wintry blast,
Her wha was here unto the last
    In heart and soul thine ain, Jamie—
    In heart and soul thine ain?

JAMIE.

Yes, I'll think o' thee when thou'rt gane, Lily—
    I'll think o' thee when thou'rt gane;
Thou'lt be my star twinkling afar
    Ower a world baith mirk and lane.
Thy bright example still will shine,
A something I can never tine;
Thy memory I'll ca' it mine
    When a' thing else is ta'en, Lily—
    When a' thing else is ta'en.

LILY.

Oh, but we've lo'ed fu' weel, Jamie—
    Oh, but we've lo'ed fu' weel;
The heavenly concord we hae had
    We baith to-day can feel.
Gin I'd to live again my life,
I'd be nae ither body's wife,
For 'mid the world's wild, weary strife
    I've found thee true as steel, Jamie —
    I've found thee true as steel.

JAMIE.

Yes, but we've lo'ed fu' weel, Lily—
    Yes, but we've lo'ed fu' weel;
Yet this, while sweet, but gars me now
    My grief the deeper feel.

You lying there upon that bed,
Seems we but yesterday were wed :
Ah ! how our married years have sped,
    Revolving like a wheel, Lily—
    Revolving like a wheel.

LILY.

Ye maunna take it sae sair, Jamie—
    Ye maunna take it sae sair ;
Since the ways of Heaven are for aye the best,
    Ye maun bravely forward fare.
O' heart and hope bate thou no jot,
Whate'er the trials of thy lot ;
Upon thee Heaven, I trow, will not
    Lay more than thou canst bear, Jamie—
    Lay more than thou canst bear.

JAMIE.

How can I but take it sair, Lily—
    How can I but take it sair ?
But thee, I'll be like a leafless tree
    In the chill and northern air.
The spring to me will be nae spring ;
The summer will nae solace bring ;
The autumn will nae fruitage hing
    Upon my boughs sae bare, Lily—
    Upon my boughs sae bare.

LILY.

Look up and trust in God, Jamie—
    Look up and trust in God ;
There's nought fa's oot without His ken
    Upon life's chequer'd road.

He sees the gait we hae to gang ;
He orders a' ; He does nought wrang ;
And in His heavenly house, ere lang,
        We'll a' hae our abode, Jamie—
        We'll a' hae our abode.

JAMIE.

I'll look up and trust in God, Lily—
        I'll look up and trust in God ;
I'll pray that His safe hand may lead
        Me aye along life's road.
Yet oh, when I nae longer see
Her whom I love, how dark 'twill be !
What human soul will then help me
        To look with hope abroad, Lily—
        To look with hope abroad ?

YOUTH.

There are who, looking back on youth, declare
    That 'twas of heaven nigh full ;
For then they seem'd to breathe more exquisite air,
    More exquisite flowers to cull ;
More exquisite air, more exquisite flowers,
O then the zephyr sweet, O then the summer bowers !

O then the morning brightness, the fresh charm,
    The world of golden sheen ;
The happy hours upon the ancient farm,
    Or sports on village green ;
The dear old home, the heartfelt greetings,
The gatherings innocent, the merry, merry meetings.

Then, too, the noble glimpses, the first sights
   Of beauty, life, and art;
The angels beckoning up the starry heights;
   The enthusiasms of the heart;
The eager, the undisciplin'd daring;
The life so frank and free; the manly, chivalrous bearing.

Yet youth is hot and restless-soul'd, and looks
   Forward too eagerly;
And halts and hindrances but badly brooks.
   Hope and despondency
Then oft by turns the heart is ruling;
And human nature then stands much in need of schooling.

Yes, human nature schooling then requires—
   O youth's hot headlong haste;
Youth's strong impelling passions and desires;
   Youth's careless, prodigal waste
Of hours and pow'rs; youth's thoughtlessnesses,
Mistakes and tumults wild, and fanciful distresses.

Give me autumnal manhood calm and fair;
   Life's Indian summer mild;
When the hush'd soul respires a heavenlier air;
   When the commotions wild
Of youth have ceas'd; when life is finer,
More dignified, more tranquil, O so much diviner!

Ah, yes; autumnal manhood, with its thought,
   Ripe, rich, and beautiful;
With its large wisdom that has been inwrought
   In life's stern training school;
Even that give me! O with the sages
Calm let me add unto the legacy of ages!

TO A DECEMBER SUN.

O sun, who, through the dull December day,
   Like to a mighty monarch in disguise,
   Hast travell'd on unto the western skies :
Now thou dost all thy glory bright display
Just when thou leav'st us.   In thy kingly way,
   Thou throw'st aside thy cloudy veil so dense,
   And turn'st to floods of brilliancy intense
The mournfullest, saddest tracts of ashen grey.
O spectacle whereon 'tis bliss to gaze !
   Yes, like yon sun I've seen a man go on,
   Sombre and dull, till life was all but gone,
Then burst into a splendid setting blaze ;
And, thus out-raying a most bright adieu,
O'er the last boundary pass away from view.

PART III

Poems on Life and Duty.

HAST THOU SEEN THE DAWNING?

HAST thou seen the dawning, so sweet and so tender,
  Breaking in on the long dark night?
Hast thou mark'd the morning's on-rushing splendour
  Put the spectral shadows to flight?

Hast thou seen the spring in blossomy glory
  And in song and rapture come in?
Yea, over the blustering winter hoary
  An easy victory win.

Hast thou perceiv'd upon land or ocean
  The fathomless peace that comes
On the back of the tempest's fierce commotion,
  When are hush'd the storm's loud drums?

Hast thou heard of honest valour quelling
  The reign of the tyrant and slave?
Hast thou heard the jubilant joy-bells telling
  Of Freedom's victories brave?

O why then, brother, art thou succumbing
  To a spirit so dastardly poor?
O why dost thou yield unto fears benumbing,
  When 'twere better to work and endure?

To a fairer world o'er Time's straits thou art sailing,
    And tho' often thy way be dark,
And the winds and the waves, a wild chaos, prevailing.
    Yet Christ's at the helm of thy bark.

Trust thou thy Pilot, and never, never
    Let the stress of things rule over thee;
By suffering stern, by manful endeavour,
    Still character fashion'd must be.

O no, our Maker is not befooling
    Us strenuous wrestlers here;
But in perfect wisdom and love is ruling,
    And the true have nought to fear.

Man! if thou art honest, if thou goest onward
    With a soul from injustice clear;
Hold up thy head, thy course is sunward,
    Thou hast simply nought to fear.

If thou doest no wrong, but doest good to thy neighbour,
    If thou helpest, not hurtest, thy friend;
If thou liv'st by reward of thy honest labour,
    Then thy life doth upward tend.

Away with the thought of a faith without practice!
    Who do His commands are the Lord's;
Yea, better, far better, one brave faithful act is
    Than myriads of high-sounding words.

Yes, at it, my brother: be more of a doer
    Of truth than thou ever hast been;
Thus truth shall, I trow, become something truer
    For thee and some more on this scene.

And murmur thou not though often impeded,
   Tho' bound in the narrowest lot;
Though thousands may seem to have better succeeded
   Whose work was less faithfully wrought.

Go on ! even the doing of commonest duty
   May mean the achievement fair
Of truth and nobleness and beauty,
   Yea, of things full rich and rare.

It is not the noisiest of successes
   That are the truest on earth ;
Nay, is it not true that God most blesses
   Who best maintains true worth ;

Who dares, in spite of prize or opinion,
   A thorough life to live ;
Who owneth only the Truth's dominion,
   And what the Truth doth give ?

PHILANTHROPY.

I YIELD high honour to the man
Who has regard to Heaven's high plan,
Nor bows to any form or rule
Of any worldly sect or school ;
Who, spite of all obstructions here,
Runs the beneficent career
Of Truth, of Mercy, and of Love,
And precept doth by practice prove ;

Whose life in whole, in part, still goes
To mitigate man's various woes,
To vanquish error, yea, to bind
With bonds of frater-love mankind.
A true child of humanity,
He cannot cold and barren be.

But thou who art more bent each day
After the world's more sordid way;
More with a worldly crust o'erlaid;
Less given thy fellow-men to aid;
Thou who hast scarce a thought to spare
To other breathers of Heaven's air;
Man! how canst thou expect a place
In the affections of thy race?
What grateful prayers, think'st thou, should rise
To waft thy name unto the skies?
What heavenly blessing should descend
To make thee rich world without end?
Thou art thine own dire enemy
Thus cold and barren here to be.

Yes, there are spots which thou may'st till;
Nooks that thou may'st with beauty fill;
Something of chaos may through thee
Order become and symmetry;
Something of lasting good be done
By thee sojourning 'neath the sun;
Something which, when thou art at rest,
May make thy weary kindred blest;
Something which doing thou may'st have
Kinship and title with the brave;

The brave, the noble toiling here,
And those high in Heaven's daylight clear.
Up, use the occasion offer'd thee !
Why should'st thou cold and barren be?

While there are mortal men to raise,
And make to live melodious days ;
Existences to lift up higher,
And with some nobler thought inspire ;
While there are darken'd minds to light
With heavenly torch of knowledge bright;
While thou with love's kind light and dew
Some parchèd spirit may'st renew ;
While thou the fires of courage high
May'st kindle in some faded eye,
And the undying blessing know
Of him or her redeem'd from woe ;
While thou such glorious good may'st see,
Why should'st thou cold and barren be ?

A SONG OF THE CITY.

THROUGH the darksome places of the city
In observant mood I take my way;
Ah, how much is here to excite heart-pity,
And what woes ne'er come to the light of day !
The tragedy here that is forward going,
The poverty, the crime, the grief,
Is past all thinking, is past all knowing,
And, could it be told, would be past belief.

L.

Yes, I say, may God bless Love's heroic endeavour,
   And each generous thing that brave spirits devise;
Yet till gold cease to lord it o'er hearts there will never
   Upspring a fair Eden to gladden our eyes.

Has earth still its thousands of vacant spaces
   Where men salubrious homes might find?
Then why in such wretched dens of places
   Crowd the sons and daughters of mankind?
O why has swelled this mighty sorrow?
   Why is it to such proportions grown?
Just because that men have not been so thorough
   In doing Christ's work as in doing their own.
Yes, I say, may God bless Love's heroic endeavour,
   And each generous thing that brave spirits devise;
Yet till gold cease to lord it o'er hearts there will never
   Upspring a fair Eden to gladden our eyes.

'Tis the thraldom of gold makes men blind to men's
     ruin;
   'Tis the thraldom of gold doth perpetuate the wrong;
Yea, 'tis this that, despite what the heroes are doing,
   Makes the good still so weak and the evil so strong.
O yes, 'tis this thraldom, this pitiful slavery,
   That more than ought else hideous evil has done;
And until to o'ercome it the race have the bravery,
   But a limited good will appear 'neath the sun.
Yes, I say, may God bless Love's heroic endeavour,
   And each generous thing that brave spirits devise;
Yet till gold cease to lord it o'er hearts there will never
   Upspring a fair Eden to gladden our eyes.

A RHYME FOR WORKERS.

WORK on! Do not flag! The true worker attains
To more than material extrinsical gains;
A character brave and a stamina strong,
Full soon unto him by his labour belong.
By his labour, perhaps by his fight for existence,
He acquires an invincible faith and persistence,
Becomes a right noble, a broad healthy man,
One moulded and wrought on a generous plan.
From the humours and crotchets of idlers he's free;
Nor patience, nor time for such folly has he!
'Tis his still to know the true glory of doing,
And laudable objects he still is pursuing;
Still toileth he on for the good of the race,
Howe'er narrow his field, howe'er humble his place;
In Humanity's march he is still pressing onward,
And, wherever you find him, his attitude's sunward.

Work on! Do not flag! Say, what mortal hath joy
Like his who his moments doth wisely employ;
Who works at the work that he finds to his hand
With what powers and resources 'tis his to command.
Who behaves him as God's and Humanity's son;
Who says, for the race let my work here be done;
Who the hewing of wood and the drawing of water
Does as well as he'd do some high dignified matter.
Who unconsciously makes his work-progress keep time
To some far-away, spirit-heard, sweet spheral chime;
Who is strong as the good and the generous are,
Who with Evil—that only—on earth doth make war.

Yes, who is so happy ?　O who has such hope,
Or who with life's trials so bravely can cope ?
Yes, work thou like such an one ! up ! do thy best,
Well earn thou the hero's immortal true rest.
So live that thro' thee there shall come some accession
To Humanity's truest and noblest possession.

Work on !　Do not flag ! and still work with a view
To increase among men the heroic and true ;
To minister good to thy kindred below,
Their joy to augment, to diminish their woe.
Macedonias around thee still loudly are crying,
And men still for lack of true wisdom are dying.
By madness are mortals to ruin still urg'd ;
And how many are here even in Britain submerg'd
'Neath poverty, darkness, and manifold crime,
In this civilis'd day, this high-privileg'd time !
Work on, work courageously, strenuously, daringly,
Yet hopefully also, O never despairingly ;
Work hopefully forward, all good is of God,
And spite of the darkness much good is abroad.
'Tis true that full oft 'tis 'mid darkening mists
Of prejudice hidden, and oft it subsists
'Mid evil entanglements ; yet we are blind,
If the precious, the noble, thro' all we don't find.
Yes, 'tis there, and if wisdom will only advise,
Or kindly assist, o'er the evil 'twill rise
In triumph and splendour—a marvellous sight,
To touch all true souls to a tearful delight.
Yes, the good in such wise may its presence assert,
Once the right word or act 'gins to play on the heart.

Yes, good is abroad, and where'er on God's earth
We wander, we need not miss finding true worth:
Ah, still we may find—not uncommon this thing—
'Neath the garb of a peasant the heart of a king;
Still the genius of song and of poesy glows
In cottages down where the primrose-flower blows;
Still those treasures resplendent, the beauties of thought
Lie in souls even from seats of fair learning remote;
Still the unction of Heaven on plain men is bestow'd;
Still herdsmen on hill-tops have visions of God.
Yes, good is abroad, the great Spirit of Good
Can ne'er be arrested, can ne'er be subdu'd;
In the silence it works and it works in the storm,
And ever its aim is to save and reform.
Thank God it is so; yes, thank God it is so;
Thank God for the bright and heroic below;
Thank God for the schemes of bright love men devise,
And for glorious ideals they'd fain realise;
Thank God for what hearts to Heaven's symphonies beat,
What souls would make life something humanly sweet;
Something humanly sweet, and adorn'd with Heaven's
    grace,
For all, for the poorest, most 'lorn of the race.

Work on, O work on! it will come, it will come,
When even like the rose the waste desert will bloom;
Yes, the idols will fall and the darkness will flee,
And the wail turn to anthems triumphant and free.
Yes, doubt thou it never, keep working, and trusting
In thy Father in heaven.   O be sure He's adjusting
Inequalities dread, and dire wrongs is redressing,
And turning harsh Marahs to rivers of blessing.

Despite the rude forces disturbing, deranging,
The purpose of God marches onward unchanging,
And nothing can happen apart from Decree
Of the Highest and Best. O when things are with
    thee
At the darkest look up to the star crown of night;
Look up to thy loadstars eternally bright.
Yes, yonder away grand and clear they are shining,
And thy dense midnight cloud has a bright silver lining.

Work on! Do not flag! Though results may come
    slowly,
O never give way to repinings unholy;
Hold one thing as settled and sure—Thou canst never
Be wholly defeated in honest endeavour.
Defeated? O never! The people defeated
Are those who from labour have shameful retreated;
Or those who have shuffled and acted deceitfully;
Or those who have scarce on the whole done less hate-
    fully—
Done nothing at all! O not with impunity
We neglect life's once-offer'd and grand opportunity.
Yes, hear me; my words now attentively mark:
The man, be he poor, be he rich, who won't work,
Who'll do nothing the while he should do what he can,
He is nought but a recreant to God and to man,
And with justice becomes he an object of scorn;
Yea, he'd better a million times ne'er have been born.
For here are we set in God's vineyard to labour,
For behoof of ourselves and our friend and our neighbour.
No, stand not aside! for the Taskmaster eyes thee,
And if thou be idle nought here justifies thee;

Not money, not rank, not position, nor any
Of the idler's most wretched excuses amany.
Yes, hopefully forward ! the good thou achievest ;
The truth that thou helpest ; the woe thou relievest ;
The misfortune that thou with thy fellow now sharest ;
The true thing, the high thing on earth that thou darest :
Of a truth all such things Son of Truth will declare thee,
And into good honour most justly will bear thee ;
Yes, many a way may conduct to futility,
But by these things thou'lt earn a most genuine nobility.

BE A MAN.

WHATSOE'ER thine earthly lot,
 Be a man ! be a man !
Foot it bravely ; falter not ;
Manlike let thy work be wrought.
Yea, with energy and thought
 Round thy plan.

Does the world with thee go hard ?
 Still endure, still endure !
Not a jot of faith discard ;
Equity and right regard ;
And the eternal bright reward
 Shall be sure.

Up ! at every hazard be
 A true soul, a true soul !
What of virtue is in thee
Keep thou that intact and free ;
Yea, maintain reality
 Sound and whole.

What and if thou canst not please
    Men in place, men in place?
Better, like old Socrates,
Drink the hemlock to the lees,
Than regard opinion's breeze
    And be base.

Thee bad triumphs would but bring
    To thy fall, to thy fall;
Thou to-day might'st be a king,
One for whom loud pæans ring,
And to-morrow a base thing
    Scorn'd by all.

See what Time to thee, Time's heir,
    Has brought down, has brought down!
High example, knowledge fair—
All in thee rich fruit to bear;
All to make thee nobly wear
    Manhood's crown!

LIFE'S JOURNEY.

I WILL never come this way again,
    I will never come back to do
One jot or one tittle left undone
    In the journey I now pursue.
The sacred duty I now neglect,
    Undone it must remain;
The unacted thought must unacted be;
    I come not this way again.

I will never come this way again;
　　Only once this journey I make;
To my precious possibilities here
　　Let me now be more awake.
The nobility that by manly acts
　　I may here and now achieve,
That let me not to some future day
　　Like a languid idler leave.

Some future day! 'tis a poor pretext;
　　Some day I may never see;
And which, if I see, will ne'er restore
　　The occasions past to me.
Some future day! 'tis a dream whereby
　　The wisest too much have lost;
O now of my God-given hours and powers
　　In God's world let me make the most.

Now let me do what things I can;
　　For why should I delay
What may now be done? ah! sufficient alone
　　For its proper work each day.
And opportunity standeth near
　　And smileth upon us sweet;
But before we know she has turn'd her head,
　　And has passed on pinions fleet.

'Tis now or never! my one life here,
　　Let me use it as I ought;
Yea, into deeds and actions fair
　　Let me quickly turn my thought.

Let me rise and quickly do the good
 I to the lov'd would do,
Lest the day should come when with bitter tears
 The unmeant neglect I rue.

No kindness to mortal let me omit
 While I have it in my power;
For I will not come this way again,
 And this is my privileg'd hour.
'Tis my privileg'd hour, and if I would be
 To God and humanity true,
I must take up my duty with master hand,
 And carry it stoutly through.

'Tis my privileg'd hour, and to use it aright
 I must feel myself a man,
And call'd by the Eternal God
 To live on a heavenly plan.
I must not worship Place or Power,
 Or play the sycophant;
I must stand erect in the fear of God,
 With a soul that nought can daunt.

My pariah brother I must own,
 My poor scorn'd sister love,
And honestly show there is help for all
 In the Christ enthron'd above.
I must go through the world with a resolute soul,
 And a heart of heavenly ruth,
And must do my best my fellows to raise
 With the levers of love and truth.

O ever to do my daily best,
  Yet never to aim too high,
For 'tis something to plant the tiniest flower
  That may cheer a poor traveller's eye.
'Tis something to give some thirsty soul
  A cooling draught to drink ;
Yes, better do this than of glorious things
  Only idly to dream and to think.

The glorious things I have dream'd and thought,
  But which I have never done,
O what, I ask, can these avail .
  To any beneath the sun ?
Let me do what my hand doth find to do ;
  Let me do it as best I can,
And still let me feel that the commonest things
  May most nobly fulfil life's plan.

I'll better act out my life's design
  By engaging my heart and my mind
To some humble task, than by striving hard
  Some chimerical good to find.
If I only let fall one seed of truth
  Which Heaven's blessing may cause to spring,
Then, I trow, to humanity's noblest wealth
  No trifling accession I'll bring.

MORNING CALL.

Up, Pilgrim, up, the morning
   Is risen, and all abroad
To conscious life returning,
   Now bow before thy God.

Give thanks for mercies shown thee
   Beyond what thou canst tell;
For goodness pour'd upon thee,
   Thou breathing miracle.

Present now thine oblation,
   In Jesus' glorious name,
Let love and adoration
   Be kindled into flame.

Reflect how Heaven's great Warrior
   From Heaven for thee came down;
Remov'd thy guilt's dread barrier,
   And grasp'd for thee the crown.

Unto His woeful passion,
   Some thoughts, O pilgrim, give;
And muse after what fashion
   Thou in this world shouldst live.

LOVE THROUGH ALL.

BLESSED are they—how fresh, how strong !
  Who, whatsoe'er misfortunes fall,
Whate'er of prejudice or wrong,
    Maintain heart-love through all.

'Tis love can make our boughs outspread,
  Can make us in rich fruits abound,
Can make us broadly, richly shed
    Light, healing dew, around.

'Tis love alone can make us know
  Life's buoyancy, life's free delight ;
Love can on mortal man bestow
    An angel's grace and might.

Love to a garden turns the heart,
  A garden full of beauty rare ;
But ah, the heart, if love depart,
    Becomes a desert bare.

Love ! it is that which makes us rich,
  Which makes the soul the chosen home
Of lovely thoughts, a place to which
    All gentle spirits come.

Love ! who can estimate its price ?
  Man ! hast thou thought what that may be ?
Could Ormus or could Ind suffice
    For love's deficiency ?

O might I celebrate love's praise !
　　Might I with glowing numbers move
Mortals deep sunk in loveless ways
　　　　To make a stand for love !

For love and all implied therein ;
　　Love's earnest faith and service free ;
Love like the Lord's, when for our sin
　　　　He went to Calvary.

'Tis love like that, invincible,
　　Whatever ills or sorrows fall,
Whose victories God Himself will tell
　　　　When He takes count of all.

Yes, love even him, the base ingrate,
　　Who doth with ill requite thy good ;
This life's fair blooms are sear'd with hate,
　　　　Stripped off with bitter feud.

But love makes life as life should be,
　　A prelude to the life above ;
That life of perfect harmony,
　　　　That life of perfect love.

Man ! throw thy petty thoughts away ;
　　Inhale a nobler atmosphere ;
Diffuse abroad love's heavenly day ;
　　　　Thus, blessing, blest be here.

Down from thy polar heights so stern,
　　Thy heights of hate and haughtiness,
Christ's stoop of love, O mortal, learn,
　　　　If thou the world would'st bless.

FOR THE RIGHT.

O BROTHER, be noble, whate'er come to pass !
Preserve thou thine honour transparent as glass ;
The rule of the Right, let that always suffice,
Still repudiate each quibble and subtle device :
Whate'er vulpine mortals may do or may say,
Be honest, be upright, be open as day.
      Go forward, my brave one !

Yes, although a wide world should aver wrong is Right,
Yea, make bold to assert that it also is Might,
Keep, keep to the line of the Right, clear and straight,
And go on spite of obstacles, many and great ;
To the Babel of tongues not one moment give heed,
But go forward where justice and honour may lead.
      Go forward, my brave one !

I ask not, I care not, how men thee describe ;
I ask not thy nation, thy kindred, or tribe ;
But I ask, Art thou here as a brave, honest man ?
Art thou seeking to live after Truth's blessed plan ?
If so, more and more a reality prove,
By justice, fair dealing, by honour and love.
      Go forward, my brave one !

Exhibit a manhood, right manly and true,
The clean thing, the right thing still valiantly do.
A shuffler or trickster still scorn thou to be ;
Act, act as one feeling there's One who doth see—
There's One who beholdeth the dwellers of earth,
And appraiseth their doings at what they are worth.
      Go forward, my brave one !

Man ! show thou art here to continue the line
Of the saints and the heroes, whose memories shine
Like bright guiding stars o'er life's labyrinth dark :
The brave who for God here on earth leave their mark :
Declare by thine actions that this is thine aim ;
Dare, dare to assert, "'Twas for this I here came !"
       Go forward, my brave one !

O something of heaven here on earth to achieve !
Some part of the sorrow of man to relieve ;
Some poor, prison'd life from its bondage to lead ;
Some fraction to meet of Humanity's need !
Yes, at it, my brother !   The brave and the true
Have much in God's world at all seasons to do.
       Go forward, my brave one !

Yes, dare to conform to the Gospel of Love ;
Yes, dare a beneficent power here to prove ;
Do not flinch ! do not bate of thy courage a jot,
Whatever the trials and straits of thy lot ;
The Right is for ever invincibly strong,
And, despite its appearances, weak is the wrong.
       Go forward, my brave one !

Afflictions may come, and misfortunes may fall :
Art thou true ? thou wilt rise up victorious o'er all ;
Have faith in thy God and thy God-bestow'd powers,
And fill up with labour the swift passing hours.
Fill them up ! Do thy noblest, thy greatest and best,
And leave to the Wisdom Divine all the rest.
       Go forward, my brave one !

WORLD-NEEDS.

THANK God for all that in this world His creatures
    Of honest, lovely, noble, say and do!
And God defend the Right and give accessions
    To the militant army of the Good and True!

The world still needs the gentle hands of Love
    To bind its immemorial wounds and bruises;
The Frys, the Nightingales, the woman-angels
    Whose heavenly presence heavenly peace diffuses.

But not the less still needs she wives and mothers
    Who'll rear up children in the fear of God;
Who'll send a Spartan and heroic offspring
    God's wide, wide earth abroad:

An offspring who, by virtue of their natures,
    Healthily moral, nobly train'd, will be
The earth's true salt, saving from putrefaction,
    And sending vigour thro' society.

The world still needs true-hearted men and valiant—
    Men who assert the whole unbiass'd mind;
Who speak straightforwardly the word of wisdom
    That they have got, in face of all mankind:

Men who thro' fair and foul march forward, forward,
    Who will not stoop to sophistries and lies
For all the kingdoms Satan ever promis'd,
    For all promotions, thrones, and dignities.

M

Men who will never let an evil flourish
   Because that evil doth prove lucrative;
Men who will hear God saying, "Go and slay it!"
   Nor heed men crying, "Spare it, let it live!"

Too much we've been the puppets of compliance,
   Souls with a shallow sense of right and wrong;
Colourless mortals, folk without conviction,
   Hence have we let the evil thing grow strong.

The world, the world still needs great John the Baptists,
   Spiritual backwoodsmen, each with axe all glittering
      keen
To lay the upas trees upon their broadsides,
   From sin's old dismal brakes to clear the scene.

Still needs she men whose meat is locusts and wild honey,
   Whose loins are leather girt, whose raiment is of camels'
      hair;
Who go forth without call of power or place or money,
   And for the King of Peace the race prepare.

Still needs she, too, the gentle Love-Apostles—
   The Johns who lean upon the Saviour's breast
And its pulsations feel—to lead her restless
   And troubled hearts into the one true rest.

Still needs she such; but infinitely various
   God's servants are, and the world needs them all;
Needs that unto her aid they should come forward
   In greater numbers, both of great and small.

Thank God for all that in this world His creatures
  Of honest, lovely, noble, say and do!
And God defend the Right and give accessions
  To the militant army of the Good and True!

LIVE A LIFE BRAVE, GENEROUS, FREE.

LIVE a life brave, generous, free,
    In thy land, in thy land.
Show what there man's life may be
In truth, wisdom, dignity,
And a blessing Heaven on thee
      Will command.

Thee, O why should Discontent
    Drive from home, drive from home?
Go not thence till thou art sent;
Work at home with large intent,
Till the blessing Heaven hath meant
      On thee come.

Ah, sayst thou, things here are not
    Moving straight, moving straight?
Man! hast thou a Godlike thought?
Into action be it wrought,
Man! to make things as they ought,
      Bend thy weight.

Work the work thou findest near
    With brave heart, with brave heart.
Man and Patriot, in thy sphere
Act, act out thy Wisdom clear ;
Without faltering, without fear,
    Do thy part.

Up! from out thy darkness spring
    At a bound, at a bound !
Make some weary heart to sing,
Light to some dark spirit bring,
Life make thou a fairer thing
    All around.

Thy best thought of life unfold
    In thy land, in thy land :
There, unspoil'd by place or gold,
Life's nobilities uphold ;
There in rich and manifold
    Forms expand.

THY FATHERHOOD IS O'ER US STILL.

THY children in the ages past
  Did stay them on Thy sovereign will,
And wheresoe'er their lot was cast
  Thy Fatherhood was o'er them still.

And we, Thy children of to-day,
  Find Thee a refuge from all ill—
A solace, an unfailing stay—
  Thy Fatherhood is o'er us still.

Yes, sure as 'Thine own Son belov'd
    Felt all our sorrows thro' Him thrill;
Sure as His death the curse remov'd,
    Thy Fatherhood is o'er us still.

Where'er through this wide world we roam,
    Whatever mandate we fulfil,
We need not feel so far from home—
    Thy Fatherhood is o'er us still.

Even 'mid the city populous,
    As by the lone sequester'd rill,
Deep felt should be this joy by us—
    Thy Fatherhood is o'er us still.

Is life like flowery meadow sweet,
    Or is it like a rocky hill
Which we must climb with weary feet?—
    Thy Fatherhood is o'er us still.

Whate'er our place or mortal state;
    Let joy or grief our spirits fill;
One thing should make us strong and great—
    Thy Fatherhood is o'er us still.

THE LOST JEWEL.

A GLORIOUS jewel once I found,
    And I was happy, I was blest;
I seem'd to tread on heavenly ground,
    'Neath heavenly suns to rest.
But soon, just like a simple boy,
I lost my jewel and my joy.

Then came my sorrows, came my griefs;
    My woes in wild battalions came;
Nor found I 'mong so-call'd reliefs
    One that was worth the name.
Nought could make up the loss; I spent
My days in search and discontent.

Yet strange it was this loss to me
    Should mean such crowding griefs and woes;
Jewels I'd left, as all might see,
    Sufficient to compose
A diadem—even ninety-nine
Bright shining jewels still were mine.

Yes, strange—yet, oh, that hundredth one
    Far more to me was than they all;
I felt that 'neath a sweltering sun
    I'd toil for years to call
It mine again. Besides, how sweet
To make my count again complete!

O restless surging of the mind!
    Still for this jewel rare I strain:
Perhaps the blind do lead the blind;
    If so, the search is vain.
Each morn I to my quest return;
Each evening sees my ardours burn.

My house have I oft swept right clean;
    Each corner I have look'd into;
To enjoy again my jewel sheen
    Nought have I failed to do
That I could think of. Memory, tell
Or where or how my loss befell!

But memory furnishes no light,
  Nothing to clear the mystery ;
And thro' the void of blind, dark night
  I grope and nothing see ;
Nothing—yet often in my dreams
I catch I know not what bright gleams.

Yes, often in my dreams methinks
  I see my jewel gleaming bright ;
And all my ravish'd spirit drinks
  Its pure and holy light :
But when I wake what grief is mine,
I only have the ninety-nine.

Oh, then, I say : "And art thou gone ?
  Or have I been the fool of nought ?
Art thou at best like fabled stone
  Philosophers have sought ?
Art thou a grand reality,
Or a golden-wingèd phantasy ?"

But wherefore thus to woe self-doom'd ?
  The precious here by God is given,
And, when it is by Him resum'd,
  'Tis waiting us in heaven.
Eureka ! there my jewel glows,
Its light my soul already knows.

FRAGMENT OF A POEM TO GENIUS.

OH, Genius, in all times hast thou stood forth
On this world-scene the impassion'd minister
Of beauty, duty, courage, hope, and love;
And all of glory, grandeur, loveliness,
And awfulness in God's great universe
Hast thou laid under tribute to thy gift.
And though ofttimes the world's Circean cup
Has brought thee down from thy far-shining heights,
Yet have thine errors—errors into which
Thou hast been plung'd by thine ardour's fierce excess—
Transfixed thee with a sorrow that has enhanc'd
Thy greatness, and to thy nobility
Added nobility.   Thy sufferings, whether
For error or for rectitude, have made
Thy voice but more authentically the voice
Of the great beating heart of humanity.
Yes, thou man's longing, labour, pain, despair,
Valour, hope, heroism hast express'd.
Now thine has been the wail of a lost world;
Now thine the voice of a glowing seraph of hope;
But whether thou hast spoken from the depths
Or from the heights of man's mysterious spirit,
Thy thrilling words have call'd forth a response
From our deep inner centre like none else.
Thy words have rung through the wide realms of thought
In long reverberations—breaking up
Our being's lethargy, emancipating
Our prison'd selves, thrilling and filling us

With glorious life; thy words have reinforc'd
The fainting heart, and rous'd the slave to burst
The degrading fetter.   Genius, thou hast been
Closely allied to Freedom in all times;
Yea, hast thou not oft stood in Freedom's van
Dauntless, equipt at once with sword and lyre?

TWO SIDES TO THE QUESTION.

Thou who wondrously art making
   Wealth, position, friends, repute;
Thou who art the world o'ertaking
   By mere dexterous speed of foot;

Great things surely thou'rt attaining,
   Yet I charge thee, do not boast!
For the world may in the gaining
   All too much, too dearly cost.

Man! think well if thou'rt not giving
   Up the glorious heritage,
Which alone makes life worth living;
   Something ample, noble, sage.

Think if thou thy higher being
   Lett'st not lie untill'd and void,
Losest not even power of seeing,
   Things God means to be enjoy'd.

The bright conquests of the ages,
   Giv'st thou unto them a thought?
Even what heroes, thinkers, sages,
   Agonisingly have wrought.

Dost thou yet perceive the spirit
   By which men were urg'd to do,
So that we might here inherit
   Things more noble, things more true?

Turn'st thou e'er aside to ponder
   What of high exalted worth,
Even what glorious moral grandeur
   Has been and is still on earth?

Yea, I ask thee—Find'st thou leisure
   For the streams, the hills, the fields?
Seek'st thou e'er that glorious treasure
   Nature to her lover yields?

With the wonder-world of nature
   Hast thou aught of unison?
Nearer, nearer thy Creator,
   Risest thou His works upon?

Unto worldly elevations
   Thou may'st mount as if on wings:
Ah, but what of aspirations
   After higher, better things?

Yes, I own thou art achieving
   Splendid world-prosperities;
But take heed thou art not leaving
   Nobler, higher things than these!

Precious inward cultivation
   Not for worlds I'd leave unsought,
Or lose sight of contemplation,
   And the power and bliss of thought.

TO A BEREAVED MOTHER.

Oh, pilgrim of Zion, why still art thou sighing,
 As if thou no more thy sweet cherubs wouldst see?
Though, like flowers of the spring, they've prov'd fading
  and dying,
 Immortal and fair, they'll be given back to thee.
Thy cherubs so fair on God's bosom are sleeping:
 Oh, wish them not back—let them rest there awhile!
For thee, weary mourner, the Lord has them keeping,
 And, with Heaven's morning-break, they upon thee will
  smile.

Look away, look away beyond dark dissolution—
 Beyond all thy griefs, and assuredly know
That thy God unto thee will make full restitution,
 And with glory outweigh all thy suffering and woe.
Oh, yield not thy soul to despair's gloomy languor;
 To Heaven's dispensations be thou reconcil'd;
Thy God doth afflict thee, but 'tis not in anger;
 'Tis the wise Heavenly Father that deals with His child.

Through grief God doth purge thee from earth's poor
  illusions,
 And out of thy darkness ordaineth thee light;
In Him put thy trust, and from direst confusions
 He will bring thee fair order and symmetry bright.
Thy Shepherd hath said, " I will never forsake thee; "
 Then say thou, with boldness, " The Lord is my stay; "
And though thou art weary and faint, He will make thee
 To leap like an hart in the heavenward way.

AN EVENING REVERIE.

WITHIN a fair lamp-lighted room
    Alone, alone I sit,
Scarce seeing forms of youthful bloom
    That past and round me flit.

Scarce marking the glad pleasantry,
    Or the gay silvery laugh
That rings from souls young, blythe, and free—
    Souls who life's nectar quaff.

I sit alone, though joys invite—
    A dream of other years
Comes o'er my soul with chequer'd light,
    And fills mine eyes with tears.

A dream of other years! Ah, why
    Am I lone dreaming now,
When happy social hearts are nigh,
    And souls with love aglow?

A dream of other years! Ah, yes;
    And other friends I see
Than those around whose fresh heart-bliss
    Rings out spontaneously.

I see a constellation fair;
    The crowd of young hearts fine,
'Mong whom 'twas mine so oft to share
    Bright social joys langsyne.

A constellation fair I see,
  And lo ! a star therein ;
A star of power and brilliancy,
  My fixed regards to win.

Then comes a thrilling voice to me,
  Which in my spirit made
A rare and wondrous melody
  Through days of light and shade.

A thrilling voice, a voice of power—
  The voice I know so well ;
The voice which did in sorrow's hour
  Of heavenly solace tell ;

The voice which in my soul would ring
  Like clarion ; ay, and make
Its depths, so deeply slumbering,
  Into responses break.

I hear it ; and Heaven's choral band
  That sweet voice also hears ;
It sings in Love's celestial land,
  And Hope dries up my tears.

A RHYME CONCERNING DUTY.

COME, thinking souls, come leave awhile this world's great
    crowded ways,
And let us meditate how we may better spend our days.
Come, let us try to muster up incentives fraught with power,
That may and ought to urge us on to use the present hour ;

To use it in such sort that we may surely be of those
Who add to the Gulf Stream of Good that down the ages
  flows.
Oh who, even the most sanguine, can too glowingly conceive
What good the humblest, meanest child may one day
  rise to achieve?
Oh who can estimate the powers wrapt in God's creature
  man,
Or the opportunity implied by this his short life-span?
Yet oft we think we are but here to toil in Mammon's
  mine,
Or 'mid gay worldly pomps and shows like dazzling stars
  to shine.
Oft we but seek to strut our day in fools' admiring sight,
And in a vain delusive show procure our sole delight.
Or it may be that we give way to pessimistic strain,
And say that effort fails its mark, that living is in vain,
That we by passion or blind chance must still be toss'd and
  driven;
That strength or guidance there is none vouchsafed us
  here by Heaven.
Thus may God's world even cease for us to be an House
  of Prayer;
Thus may this human life become a dogged, blank despair.
Yea, in this case we may give way to godless revelry;
Let us eat and drink, let us merry be, for to-morrow we
  shall die.
Or we may doleful lie beneath the weight of our sad state,
As if there were not but ourselves here to compassionate.
And all the while we verily would, if we had eyes to see,
Find those even at our very doors more wretched far than
  we;

Those upon whom we fitly might some friendly thought
    bestow,
And by so doing through the world the lighter, freer go.
Alack that we should all the world but our small inch for-
    get,
And we in very deed "a part of all whom we have met."
O men! O women! if we would but think what would
    accrue
Unto the world and to ourselves from the least that we
    could do;
That we could do in decency, in this our God-given day,
For our fellows here, then we would rise, then we would
    rise, I say,
And would forth in the name of Love and Truth, in the
    name of Highest God,
And would tread the shining, glorious path that the heroes
    here have trod.
O men! O women! let us live as those should live who're
    born
A God of love to glorify, and this His world to adorn;
His world to adorn, to do our part to meet the race's need,
And into fairer, brighter paths our kindred here to lead.
O men! O women! let us share the loads that galling press
Poor human hearts; yea, let us try to make our plague-
    spots less.
Our plague-spots? Yes, are there not such existing still on
    earth?
And to destroy them should we not put our best efforts
    forth?
Is it not said concerning Him who was God's Son most
    blest
That He the devil's works to spoil was here made manifest?

O blessed they whose lives like His are here a strong
    crusade
Against all darkness, they by whom this scene is nobler
    made;
They who industrious seek to fill their place in God's high
    plan;
They who still lead man up to God and bring God down
    to man;
They who accept the very work that lieth to their hand,
And carry it thro' with all the powers their being can com-
    mand;
They who go onward, valiant, wise, noble, serene, and free,
Still giving indications bright of what man's life should be;
Life's rich occasions using up as nearly to the full
As mortals may, achieving still the true, the beautiful.
Let no one say there comes no strength nor guidance from
    on high,
For everything most sure is ours that mercy can supply.
Thank God that we can make this life a thing beneficent,
And feel that 'twas for good, not ill, that we were hither
    sent.
Thank God that fountains pure of joy within our hearts
    arise,
When we for fellow-creatures here brave, liberal things
    devise;
Brave, liberal things devise, and as our wisdom may
    direct,
Project them forth into the world, give them most blest
    effect.
Thank God for all the encouragement which He to us has
    given,
That we may work to make the earth a little liker heaven.

Thank God for infinite good! But why from well-doing
    hold me back,
And life so passing, too, and night so soon upon our track?
A little while, and on this earth, with its fair dome the skies,
On every dear familiar sight we close our mortal eyes;
We'll see no more the goodliness of the lovely varied year,
And the generations o'er our graves will tramp, but we will
    not hear.
A little while at longest, short the space we here abide,
And set beside the Eternal scene. poor, poor Earth's pomp
    and pride.
What is it worth, yon equipage, yon noisy, vain display?
The wise man, far above it all, keeps calmly on his way.
So let us live as those should live on whom God has conferr'd
Honour and blessing, those for whom good things have
    been prepared;
Those who are here the lawful heirs of Time's vast legacy
Of knowledge, wisdom, types of worth and high nobility;
Those who have here with prayerful faith Love's duty to dis-
    charge
To those at home, to those far off, yea, to the world at
    large;
Those who can look as kings and priests thro' Nature's
    realm abroad,
Knowing that they o'er all these things have been ordained
    by God;
Those for whose joy this scene was made so glorious and
    so bright;
Those unto whom field, hill, and grove do minister delight.
So shall we surely bless mankind, and truly honour God;
And Joy and Peace shall go with us, and sweeten all our
    road.

OH, PILGRIM! FOR WHOM A BRIGHT CITY ETERNAL.

OH, Pilgrim! for whom a bright City Eternal
    Is the end of thy journeyings here,
I advise that, while on through earth's mystery thou farest,
Thou take heed that to all men thyself thou still bearest
    With a soul at once just and sincere.

    I advise that thou break through all trammels sectarian
    If thou wouldst thy fellows improve:
Recollect that beyond thine own circle are others
Who, in deed and in truth, are thy sisters and brothers,
    And have therefore a claim on thy love.

    I advise that thou act with a love broad and generous,
    Nor into disputings to fall;
Rather rescue the souls that in misery welter;
Rather bring men within the secure heavenly shelter
    Of that love that has conquer'd for all!

    I advise that thou labour to raise up thy species
    To their glorious, their God-design'd place:
Ah, thou wilt be blest while thou others art blessing,
And while spending thyself wilt thyself be increasing,
    For 'tis thus in the Kingdom of Grace!

GOD'S LOVE.

OH, Heavenly Love, from heaven still stooping down,
Each day Thou dost our lives with blessings crown.
    I will praise Thee, O God; I will praise Thee
      For Thy love, constant still and sublime;
    Thy love is a theme for eternity:
      'Tis all too vast for time.

What time we fall, angels of love draw nigh
To lift us up, and point us to the sky.
    I will praise Thee, O God; I will praise Thee
      For Thy love, constant still and sublime;
    For Thy love is a theme for eternity:
      'Tis all too vast for time.

In peace He blesses us, in trouble saves,
Yea, holds us up above the swelling waves.
    I will praise Thee, O God; I will praise Thee
      For Thy love, constant still and sublime;
    Thy love is a theme for eternity:
      'Tis all too vast for time.

NEW YEAR.

Now step with reverence upon
    This untrodden tract of time,
And foot it bravely, bravely on,
    To Hope's triumphant chime.
The future!—who can know it?
    Let it smile or let it low'r;
Comrades! 'tis only given us
    To live from hour to hour.

NIL DESPERANDUM.

COURAGE, my brother! wherefore low views taking?
    There's more to raise thee up than to depress;
There's an invincible spirit here still making
    For beauty, mercy, truth, and righteousness.

Even where we least expect, some moral beauty,
    Like to a lovely glimpse of heaven, appears;
Some instance of brave love, and faith, and duty
    Flashes upon us, touching us to tears.

Let us go forward with love-lighted faces,
    Dethroning with God's weapons hoary wrong;
Planting Heaven's precious seed in earth's dark places,
    Teaching the wastes to break forth into song.

THE HIGHLAND CROFTER.

OCHON, ochrie! and must I sail
    To lands far ower the main,
And on my bonnie Highland hills
    Set foot nae mair again?
Can Highland hills nae mair support
    My wife and bairns and me?
Hae we nae mair a right therein?
    Ochon, ochon, ochrie!

Our ancestors, in auld grey times—
    Sae much, at least, I ken—
Were station'd in their Highlands grand,
    A race o' valiant men.

And they had chieftains leal and strong,
  Whose love they still possess'd ;
And they were bound in clanship's bands,
  With proud clan feelings blest.

And cattle, sheep, and deer had they,
  And produce of the kine ;
And fish and fowl were aye at hand
  Whereon my sires might dine.
Braw Highland folks did then, I trow,
  Possess their Highlands grand ;
For wha, O wha could then drive forth
  The children of the land ?

But times are changed : our Highlands grand
  Now less and less belong
To Highland folks ; for now, alas !
  We are nae langer strong.
We're broken now, and turn'd the prey
  Of greed and power's demand ;
Yea, strangers say to us, " Give place,
  And yield to us the land !

" Yield up the land ; 'tis yours no more ;
  'Tis bought with honest gold ;
Give place, give place ! to the last mite
  The price we down have told."
And, if we should refuse to go,
  Then Law must take its course ;
And forth we maun be driven like sheep
  By harsh eviction's force.

It's O my fathers' ancient land,
   So rugged, wild, and stern ;
Thou land where hoary legends hang
   Round castle, crag, and cairn ;
Thou land which bards and heroes rear'd,
   My own belov'd countree ;
That thine own children thus should cease
   To hae a part in thee !

It's O my bonnie rush-clad hame
   Upon the loch's lone shore ;
Dear hame from which my parents' dust
   We to the kirkyaird bore ;
Thou lovely scene, to me endear'd
   By memories o' langsyne,
Scene aye my ain, alack that thou
   Must be nae langer mine !

Ochon, ochrie ! yes, I must sail
   Across the ocean wide ;
For now there's less and less for them
   Wha in their land abide.
Nae mair can Highland hills support
   My wife and bairns and me ;
We hae nae mair a right therein—
   Ochon, ochon, ochrie !

TO A MOURNING BROTHER.

WEEP, brother, at thy helpmeet's grave with unavailing
   sorrow,   [to-morrow.
'Tis dark with thee to-day ; perchance 'twill darker be
Thy hollow void of loss may then more painfully be aching ;
Thy heart, thy poor bereaved heart, more cruelly abreaking.

And thou mayst ask, " What good is toil since she who
    still could cheer me
No more will beautify the scene or hover gaily near me?
What good the wish'd success since she no more with me
    can share it?
What good the victor's wreath since now she cannot see
    me wear it?"

And thou mayst sit for days and nights within thy lone-
    some dwelling,
Oblivious of the circling hours the household clock is
    telling;
Thy life's fair object's gone to nought; thy purpose all
    confounded;
Thy soul in depths far deeper plung'd than ever plummet
    sounded.

Yet thou at length must rise and do, must up and on be
    marching,
Some happy, worthy end in view; yon blue heaven o'er
    us arching,
This flowery earth—all speak of hope! and in life's brave
    endeavour,
Thou, thou, thy good, thy hope must find tho' *she* is gone
    for ever.

LOVE IS MORE THAN GOLD.

TRUE, most true, I still have found it —
    Let me say't to young and old!
That howe'er we lightly wound it,
    Love is more than Gold.

For Love's hurt or ruination,
   Not the vastest sum e'er told
Can suffice as reparation—
   Love is more than Gold.

Gold can rear a stately palace ;
   Can do wonders manifold ;
Love alone can fill life's chalice—
   Love is more than Gold.

Homage, suffrage, and opinion—
   Yes, I own even they are sold ;
Yet, though great is Gold's dominion,
   Love is more than Gold.

Mine is no position brittle,
   I in this am strong and bold ;
Love that makes us blest with little,
   That is more than Gold.

Go thy way, thou sordid-minded,
   To thy mammon-creed still hold ;
But 'tis true—thou yet mayst find it—
   Love is more than Gold.

Yet the human hearts around thee
   May turn interested, cold,
And the solemn truth may wound thee—
   Love is more than Gold.

Wheresoe'er we may be faring,
   Life this truth doth still unfold ;
Suffering hearts are still declaring,
   Love is more than Gold.

Furious mammonite contentions,
    Griefs in tearful torrents roll'd,
Force on our dull comprehensions—
    Love is more than Gold.

THE SUN OF RIGHTEOUSNESS.

THERE is a Sun, the sent of God,
    Which earth's dark clouds has riven;
Which pours in majesty abroad,
    The holy light of heaven.
It is this Sun, this blessed Sun,
    Whose beams the stricken heal,
Whose steady light conducts us on
    To our eternal weal.

O peerless Sun of Righteousness,
    From thee such sweetness flows,
As makes the dreary wilderness
    To blossom like the rose.
Thou dost dissolve the stubborn yoke
    Of darkness and despair,
And wealth of flowers and fruits evoke
    Upon life's furrows bare.

Yet ours is death's dark mournful reign,
    Whate'er our state now seems,
If still impervious we remain
    Unto Thy living beams.

Creation's hope !   This dark world's light,
    Light wherein light we see ;
O, why should any walk in night,
    All blind and dull to Thee ?

Why, when God's Spirit would anoint
    The dull eyes of our mind,
Will we that Spirit disappoint,
    And still be wilful blind ?
For most part 'tis because we'd have
    Our good things on the earth,
And disbelieve, while these we crave,
    In things of heavenly worth.

We plume us on the mighty store
    That here to us doth fall,
And feel not we are wretched, poor,
    Blind, naked, needing all.
By semblances we're captive led,
    We see the present hour,
And bless who lift on high the head,
    And much have in their power.

Poor, flaunting souls, we happy call,
    Men of this world count great ;
So recreant are we grown to all
    That lifts our fallen state ;
So wilfully we're lacking sight
    For what alone can bless,
And make us great—the world's true light,
    The Sun of Righteousness.

O once I was a wayward child,
    I had no guiding ray,
By glittering phantoms, marsh-fires wild,
    I far was lur'd astray.
I thought earth's better good to find,
    And broken cisterns tried,
Till disappointed, 'wilder'd, blind,
    To God for light I cried.

Light came; God's Spirit to mine eyes,
    God's cleansing salve applied;
I look'd, God's Sun was in my skies,
    The Saviour who had died.
The Lord who stoop'd in mercy low,
    That all our ills might cease,
The risen Sun whence ever flow
    Life, healing, love, and peace.

And now, O Lord, I know Thou art
    Indeed a Sun and Shield
To every poor and stricken heart
    Who to Thy love will yield.
And I would in Thy light go on,
    And, bless'd, would others bless,
And say to some, behold the Sun,
    The Sun of Righteousness!

O Sun, by whom God's precious grace
    A free salvation brings;
Sun who can pierce the darkest place,
    With healing in Thy wings:

Might scales of ignorance and sin
  From each dark spirit fall,
Might Thy celestial light shine in,
  Illuminating all.

———— ——

HEAR ME, GIVER OF ALL BLESSING!

HEAR me, Giver of all blessing!
Should I e'er, Thy gifts possessing,
  Feel no need of Thee;
Should even blessings blind my spirit,
Till I see not my demerit—
  Christ, remember me!

Or, should worldly sights alluring
Come between me and the enduring
  Too bewitchingly;
Should earth show too much profusion
Of enchantment and illusion—
  Lord, remember me!

Or if driven by gales of passion
I be ready even to dash on
  Rocks of misery;
When I'm yielding, when I'm reeling
With tumultuous thought and feeling—
  Christ, remember me!

Or should falsehood or oppression
Mar my peace and self-possession,
  Bruise me cruelly;

Should my heart be torn and bleeding
Loving Saviour interceding—
   Lord, remember me!

Or if called to suffer trial
Of sore mockery and denial
   For the truth and Thee;
Should I fool's reproach be bearing,
Or Thy prickly chaplet wearing—
   Christ, remember me!

Or should earth be turning dreary
Through the many changes weary
   Thou dost bid me see;
Through the going home of lov'd ones,
Loyal-minded, tried, and prov'd ones—
   Lord, remember me!

Or should come my last affliction,
And therewith the stern conviction,
   This mine end must be;
Should death's darkness be appalling,
Yea, should deep to deep be calling—
   Christ, remember me!

BEFORE THE GODHEAD.

BEFORE the Godhead we our lives transact;
The Heavens do look and see us live and act;
As by the Eternal Powers beheld,
Let every man now plough and sow his field.

LET THE DREAMER WHO HATH NEVER.

LET the dreamer who hath never been 'mid the whirlwinds
    of passion
Talk of a perfect creed and life—far other be thy fashion !
In the thick of the battle of life, where so many strong are
    o'erthrown—
There, 'gainst the devil, the world, and the flesh, be it thine
    to hold thine own !

AN EPITAPH.

STOP, passer ! She whose dust here lies walk'd earth with
    reverent feeling ;
And, in her few steps up to God, God's light was still
    revealing :
Her life was after the high plan of God's own blest
    evangel ;
And still she was to him she lov'd a bright and guardian
    angel.

THOU ART COME!

Now my path will be thy path here; my abode be thine
    abode ;
And ours will be one people, one altar, and one God ;
Thou wilt never, never leave me ; thou wilt never bate one
    jot
Of thy grand and true devotion, whatsoe'er may be our lot.
        Thou art come ! thou art come !

Now I rise to higher objects, with a higher zeal I'm fir'd ;
With a nobler, freer spirit is my spirit now inspir'd ;
Up to bright divine ideals now my ardent soul doth yearn,
And, from life's broad page sun-smitten, deeper, vaster
    things I learn.
       Thou art come ! thou art come !

Now I scorn these vulpine methods ; I eschew this vulgar
    strife ;
A true purpose, at all hazards, I will carry into life ;
Lords and gods of gold and substance let others strive to be,
I choose a better warfare and a nobler part with thee.
       Thou art come ! thou art come !

Now I gird my loins for battle, for the grand ennobling fight ;
For humanity's sore conflict, for the cause of God and
    right ;
I am now myself twice over ; I will forth and do and dare
And of no good, no conquest will I henceforth despair.
       Thou art come ! thou art come !

A MAIDEN'S STORY.

SOME human lives are shadowed soon—
Shadow'd was mine long, long ere noon ;
Yet O that blessed morning time
When 'twas as bright as sunny clime ;
When he I lov'd was with me found
Like an angel on terrestrial ground ;
That time when he was everything—
A fountain clear, a joyous spring.

A shield, a covering o'er my head,
In love most true, most tender spread.
O ne'er will I forget that time!
Yet not of that in this my rhyme
Would I descant. I now must tell
How with the man I lov'd so well
It soon turn'd out; how he discarded
His faith in what he'd once regarded
As of ineffable sacredness;
And how from that came our distress:
Yea, many a year of misery
And grievous pain to him and me.

Yes, there are sorrows worse than death
And the renouncement of our faith
In God's eternal verities
Is surely not the least of these.
Ah, 'twas with sharpest pang of grief
That I first mark'd that his belief
In holy Christian truth was failing,
And that he shortly might be sailing
Away on I knew not what wild seas
Of scepticisms and falsities!
With pang, I well might say heart-rending,
I marked an awful woe impending.
Then my life was wholly smitten dim
When he told me plainly that in him
A change had gradually been wrought—
A change which he had never sought;
Nay, in incipiency had hated,
And loath'd, and fear'd, and deprecated;

A change which, since 'twas hard to resist,
He thought was likely to persist;
A change which much he fear'd would be
To me a cause of misery;
For unto him it meant just this—
That he no longer must profess
The faith in which he'd been baptiz'd,
The old, the once-lov'd faith of Christ.

'Twas in such wise to me he show'd
What I constru'd his lapse from God;
His lapse from God and Him who died
The door of hope to open wide.
Then forthwith he began to state
The things that now with him had weight—
The things, alas! his soul had wed
In the most blessed Saviour's stead.
He had embrac'd some splendid *ism*
Which meant for me bold scepticism,
Even a denial flat of all
That I'd been wont the truth to call.
Bright phantasies he had embrac'd;
In cobwebs of the brain had plac'd
His trust—had taken husks instead
Of Christ, the true and living bread.
'Twas an unlooked-for, woeful change;
'Twas a perversion passing strange
Beyond all that I could have thought
Could be on one so noble wrought.
So noble! Yes, so noble he,
A king 'mong men he seem'd to be:

High dignity and manly grace
Mark'd out alike his form and face;
And his mind was full of the sublime
Grand harmonies of ancient time;
Yea, what had down the ages come
Of grandeur found with him a home.

Yes, a dire weight upon me press'd;
And I was mightily distress'd
While I beheld this noble one
So led astray and so undone.
He who such things might have achiev'd,
He to be thus misled, deceiv'd
By streams of sceptic influences
And philosophic vain pretences!
And then to think of the consequences!
O must my darling idol fall
Down from my soul's fair pedestal?
Ah! fain would I have kept him there,
Therefore I gave myself to prayer
On his behalf; and often spoke
With him, and tried to break the yoke
Of dismal error.   Ah, in vain,
God, God alone could break his chain,
Or unweave the net where he was ta'en;
Where though a woeful captive he
Was voluble of liberty;
Of liberty and dreams of hope
To work out which the world gave scope—
Bright dreams with which I could not cope.
Yes, God alone must him convert—
Meantime, alas! we two must part—

A stern, a sore necessity,
Whether I would or not, on me
Was laid. With him I now must break,
Since he his awful road would take;
Since, 'stead of Christ he now would follow
Poor phantoms and delusions hollow.

No! 'twas not to be thought that thus
Things should just take their course with us.
How, how could I have aught to do
With one who had plainly left the true
And Scriptural way our fathers trod—
The way unto the City of God?
With sorrow more than I can tell
At length I said to him farewell:
I said farewell—I had a fight
Ere I could say it, but 'twas right.
Nay, 'twas no more than just obeying
What Heaven's own voice had long been saying
Deep in my soul—" My daughter, see
You be not yok'd unequally !"
'Twas right, 'twas right ! my course was clear,
Though it cost me many a pang and tear
To accept it. Many a day and night
Of grief had I, though it was right.
Who knows what sorrows we must have
Between the cradle and the grave ?

Years pass'd; yes, since that dreadful day
When I said farewell, and he went his way,
His way of lonely grief and woe,
Or what I thought would soon be so.

Since then of years a long, long train
Pass'd ere I saw his face again ;
Ah, years to me of anxious care
And sorrow, O so hard to bear !
Him from my heart I sought to expel,
And tried each thought of him to quell
As it uprose; but 'twas in vain
So long as memory would retain
Its mighty power.   During the day
I pictur'd him upon his way
Alone ; and in the night I dream'd
That I beheld him.   Then he seem'd
A man of woe.   Along a road,
Rugged and dark, he bore a load—
A load that look'd just like to bring
Him to the earth ; for, staggering
And feebly reeling, on he went,
As if his strength was all but spent.
"O God !" I cried, "might I but bear
Of his dire load the smallest share !"
Yet was he burden'd ?   Not a word
Of good or bad from him I heard :
Nay, nor to that had I a right,
Since I had sent him from my sight.

I knew he threaded life's weary scene ;
But a great gulf yawn'd our souls between ;
And till the Lord should bring him back
From wandering on yon fatal track,
Oh, what had I to do with him ?
Yes, life with me was smitten dim ;

My life was dim, or even dark;
Or like something that had miss'd its mark;
Yea, wretched, wretched was my state;
Yet 'twas my duty still to wait
In silence and in patience on
Till the work by God should be wholly done.

Therefore I waited and I waited,
As in some desert one belated
Might wait the dawn, with nought but God
To save him from wild beasts abroad.
'Tis true, the beasts that menac'd me
Were only fears; yet dreadfully
Could these assail.   A time it was
When thro' thick darkness I'd to pass;
Yet oft upon the steps of prayer
I seem'd to reach the perfum'd air
Of Heaven; and then resign'd and blest
I'd say, "The Lord He knoweth best
The things we need, and often here
Is kindest when He's most severe!"
Such times were mine; yet as oft I cried,
Like an orphan'd thing thro' the world wide.

Oh, how it came I scarce can tell;
But One there is who knows right well,
Even He whose blest beneficence
Still meets us in His providence;
Even He who holds in His own hand,
In every place, on sea and land,
This strangely tissu'd web of things;
Even He beneath whose mighty wings

His people trust, His people wait,
Whate'er their sorrow or their strait.
Yes, well He knows how 'twas we met,
For time and place by Him were set!—
When many a weary year had pass'd,
When Hope into her tomb seem'd cast—
Cast, never more to rise again—
When prayer itself seem'd well-nigh vain,
'Twas then my sore extremity
Became God's opportunity;
'Twas then, 'mid life's strange chequer'd maze,
Yea, as 'mid sun-forsaken days,
I met him, and I fell on his breast,
And our tears were mingled and we were blest.

Yes, it had come, had come at last;
His wild delusions now were past,
Those dreams unsanction'd and unblest
In which no soul could find its rest;
Those gorgeous-gay extravagances
That shone as if with bright sun-lances;
Those outbursts of unsober hope;
Those things with which I could not cope
God had withstood.   Now he was free
With a holy Christian liberty.
Free!—yes, with glorious jubilations
Might angels from their heavenly stations
Announce—Another soul is free!
Free! free!—Yet who unmov'd could see
How much his wanderings had cost;
How much thereby was marr'd and lost?

Who having known him in the old years
Could now behold him without tears?
He was like one who had been cast
On evil days; one who had pass'd
Through trials sore; through ordeals dire,
As wracking storms, or scathing fire.
Yea, it was plain that death would come
Ere many days to take him home.

With anxious thoughts, I heard him speak—
Alack, his voice was low and weak.
He told me how the dreams he cherish'd
Had, wanting heavenly sustenance, perish'd;
How the life that he had thought to live
Could never for an instant give
True satisfaction to his soul—
How still he seem'd to miss his goal;—
Yea, how the schemes that he had thought
To fashion forth had gone for nought;
How to the ground he'd seen them fall
Poor, useless, and utopian all!
How his bread had been steep'd in bitter tears
Thro' many dark and feverish years;
And he had found no rest, no rest,
Nor in any work or way been blest!—
Such was the tenor of his speech:
Then he told me how the Lord did reach
A hand to him when prostrate he
Was lying 'neath his misery.

I scarce need say that to the end
I did myself on him attend.

A few short days of hallow'd feeling
We two enjoyed; then death came stealing,
Came stealing like a wavelet on,
And ere I knew it, he was gone.
Ah me! could yon indeed be death
That pal'd his beauty's fragile wreath?
Yes, yes, 'twas death; and when he lay
Within the gloaming's shadows grey
Silent and cold, a lingering grace
Still shining on his marble face,   .
I thought of him as blest and free,
And the sight was solemn-sweet to me:
'Twas solemn-sweet; 'twas grand; for O
Well did I feel, well did I know
That 'mong the ransom'd and the blest
Another wanderer was at rest.

THE STREET PREACHER.

In the centre of the market,
    In the balmy summer night;
See, see where he is standing,
    Yon strange and hoary wight;
Standing up with his head uncover'd,
    With his hat in his left hand;
With his right hand high uplifted
    With an air of sublime command.
Yet his attitude, too, is attractive,
    Even while it inspireth awe;
And the people on the market
    Slowly around him draw.

Yes. look at him ! he is formèd
　　On no less than herculean plan ;
And one might almost judge him
　　Some old Covenanter-man.
Yes, his eye is like the eagle's,
　　And his locks are like the snow ;
While his shaven cheek like the rowan
　　Of autumn seems to glow.
And his forehead is broad and lofty,
　　And clearly cut his face ;
And the old man altogether
　　Has about him a wondrous grace.
But mark him now ! he a little
　　His right hand down has brought ;
And hark ! he speaks ; and the people
　　By the spell of his voice are caught.
Oh, the wailing, wailing accents !
　　Who, who can these resist ?
Ah, surely this man has been nurtur'd
　　'Mong the hills, in the storm, and the mist !
'Tis silence deep around him,
　　He only the silence breaks ;
Let me try to report the substance
　　Of what the old preacher speaks :—

SERMON.

Ho, my brother ! ho, my sister !
　　Fellow-mortal, unto thee
I speak—vouchsafe an audience ;
　　Hearken awhile unto me !

In a little 'twill matter little
    Whether thou wert peasant or peer;
But much it will matter whether
    Thou didst do thy duty here—
Much it will matter whether
    Thou wert God's and Humanity's friend;
Whether for Truth's upholding
    Thy labours here did tend;
Whether a man or a woman
    Of convictions true thou wert;
Whether the weal of thy fellows
    Thou didst seek with all thy heart.
Yes, much it will matter whether
    Thou were here right-hearted, brave;
Or only a colourless mortal,
    A vacillating slave.
'Tis a thing of solemn import,
    This life we now transact;
Wilt thou make it a something amorphous,
    Or a sternly shapen fact?
O mortal, it lieth now with thee
    To let it be shamefully marr'd,
Or to painfully shape it to something
    Which thy Maker with joy will regard.
Say, what's thy moral fibre?
    Art thou honest? art thou true?
Then fear not to stand forward,
    And to do what lies to do.
Up, up! for time is passing;
    Up, and gird thee for the fight;
For the grand heroic conflict,
    For the battle for the right.

Hast thou this world consider'd?
　Hast thou seen it with vision clear?
Hast thou mark'd the struggling and striving
　For a little elbow-room here?
The struggling, the striving, the wrestling
　For a little money or place;
The headlong pell-mell running,
　The hurry-skurrying chase?
Hast thou mark'd the clash of ambitions,
　The rancour and the strife;
And how brotherly-kindness so often
·　Is shoulder'd out of life?
Hast thou seen how honour is trodden
　By unprincipled self in the dust,
And how oftener we find a professor
　Than a man who is strictly just?
Hast thou mark'd the vulpine methods,
　The chicanery, the pretence,
And the reaving, and robbing, and spoiling
　Of simple innocence?
Hast thou seen all this? Hast thou thought, too,
　Of the ruins of lust and drink?
O, my brother, these things are dreadful,
　Beyond what the heartless think!
O the souls made in God's image,
　Whelm'd and lost on misery's seas;
And so many—O, so many—
　Dwelling in Zion at ease!
A brave band, I deny not, are toiling
　To meet the world's great need:
Yet, O the crowds of self-centred
　That pass on and give no heed!

Up, up! for time is passing:
   Up and gird thee for the fight;
For the grand heroic conflict,
   For the battle for the right.

Man! is it for wrangling and haggling
   On the busy marts of trade?
Is it for money-making
   That thou wert merely made?
Is this thy *summum bonum*,
   To clutch the greatest share
Of the prizes that are going
      n the world's great mammon fair?
Is thine aim to get together
   A spendid heap of pelf,
And to build a lordly mansion
   Wherein to enjoy thyself?
O man! there is something better
   To which thou may'st give heed:
'Tis to see that, whate'er thy condition,
   Thou meet part of the world's great need;
'Tis to walk in God's beauteous order,
   To fulfil sweet mercy's plan,
To work for thy sister-woman,
   To work for thy brother-man.
There are are still great wrongs to be righted,
   Huge evils to redress;
And we all may reclaim a portion
   Of the howling wilderness.
There are unstanch'd wounds, sharp sorrows,
   For which something may be done;
There is work, my brother, my sister,
   For each of us 'neath the sun.

It's O just a word of wisdom
   At the time and place to speak,
Just a solace to give to the weary,
   Just a cup of strength to the weak.
Up, up! for time is passing,
   Up and gird thee for the fight,
For the grand heroic conflict,
   For the battle for the right.

Am I my brother's keeper?
   It was Cain, the fratricide,
That ask'd the selfish question—
   Wilt thou be with Cain allied?
Wilt thou turn away, cold-hearted,
   From thy brother and sister's case?
Wilt thou close thine eyes on the sorrow
   That stares thee in the face?
Nay, nay! for truth, for mercy,
   For love, take then thy stand;
Deny thyself and follow
   Thy Lord—'tis His command.
Man! hast thou never ask'd thee
   Why it is that here thou art?
Hast thou never felt a mission
   Burning hot within thy heart?
A mission of love and aidance
   Entrusted by High Heaven
To thee, to thee—O marvel!
   And not to an angel given;
A mission which thou, God's servant,
   Must do at every cost;
Must do, and that right quickly,
    Lest thy golden day be lost.

Man ! think what thou wilt of existence,
　　Yea, bathe it in hues of romance,
I tell thee it has an awful,
　　A most dread significance.
The claims of Heaven are upon thee,
　　And the claims of humanity,
And not with impunity canst thou
　　Put any the least of them by.
Up, up ! for time is passing ;
　　Up and gird thee for the fight,
For the grand heroic conflict,
　　For the battle for the right !

The veteran preacher's voice now dies away—
He pauses ; yet 'tis plain he more would say.
After a minute's thought he opes again
His mouth ; but now he chants a different strain :
This time he is the rapt evangelist—
What sinner now the claims of Jesus shall resist ?

SECOND SERMON.

Thou art still under death's iron rule, sinner,
　　If Christ has not enter'd thy heart ;
Though loved and caress'd, thou canst not be bless'd
　　While thou with the Lord has no part.
O think of thy case, as a stranger to grace,
'Mong God's blessed children thou hast not a place.

Of gems from Philosophy's mine, sinner,
　　Or of parentage high thou may'st boast ;
Thou mayest have wealth, genius, beauty, and health,
　　But while Christ is not thine thou art lost.
Not the sum of earth's gold, nor yet talents untold,
Can purchase an entrance to Christ's blessed fold.

But Christ may be thine e'en to-day, sinner,
  There is life through His death now for thee;
Thou art lost and undone, but for thee God's dear Son
  Has groan'd, bled, and died on the tree.
The best gifts of God are on rebels bestow'd;
Now more than man lost is made free by Christ's blood.

The Saviour now calls upon thee, sinner,
  To partake of His rich feast of grace;
No plea nor excuse have those who refuse,
  For the feast is for all our lost race.
Jesus' promise is sure, both for rich and for poor,
His blood unto all men has op'd Mercy's door.

Even now thou may'st hunger no more, sinner,
  Christ's banquet for thee is now spread;
Then come to the board of Heaven's gracious Lord,
  And abundantly eat of Life's bread.
Come, sinner, and prove Jesus' kindness and love
To the Zion below and the Zion above.

Why labour and sigh for earth's joys, sinner?
  Your substance for nought wherefore pay?
At the Saviour's feet now thy rest may be sweet,
  There Heaven may be thine e'en to-day.
There, there is relief from sin and from grief,
Tho' of sinners or mourners thou may'st be the chief.

O why should'st thou thirst any more, sinner,
  Thou art now on Life's limpid stream's brink,
Life's stream flows for thee, unto all it is free,
  Stoop down, weary sinner, and drink.
Drink, drink, fever'd one, till thy fever is gone,
Here, here in this world true refreshment is known.

Thy Maker now seeketh thy heart, sinner,
　　Thou wert made for this glorious end—
To tread wisdom's ways, in the garments of praise,
　　And commune with thy God and thy Friend.
O why life employ, seeking brief mingled joy,
While yours may be bliss without end or alloy?

By Nature's ascriptions of praise, sinner;
　　By her glory beyond that of art;
By the triumphs of grace, achieved 'mong our race,
　　God calls thee to give Him thy heart.
While His call men refuse, sovereign grace they abuse,
And the way to eternal destruction they choose.

By the mercies of every new day, sinner,
　　By trials, by grief's bitter smart;
By his servants and Word, thy Creator and Lord
　　Now asks thee to give Him thy heart.
Why labour and plan, as if frail, dying man
Had all that concerned him in life's little span?

God's claim thou canst never annul, sinner;
　　All thou hast—body, soul, heart, and mind—
Unto Jesus belong; O then cease to do wrong;
　　Yield them all to the Friend of mankind.
Cease to wrong the Most High; cease, poor sinner, to die;
By the blood of Atonement to God now draw nigh.

O ne'er canst thou glorify God, sinner,
　　Till thou yield to the Saviour's high claim;
'Tis in choosing the Lord, that men first accord
　　The praise that is due to God's name.
Only then can we know true enjoyment below;
Only then from God's favour our pleasures can flow.

Sin's leprosy reigns in thy soul, sinner,
    Yet doubt not Christ's love, will, and power;
He slays sin and death, in Him now have faith,
    And thou shalt be heal'd from this hour.
Health of soul shall be thine, and Heaven's beauty divine,
Though thy garb may be poor and thy body may pine.

As the leper was banish'd afar, sinner,
    From man's dwellings, so, be thou assur'd,
Thou an outcast shalt be, nor God's fair city see,
    If thy deadly disease is not cured.
But to-day may thy soul be cleans'd and made whole,
And, rejoicing in God, may press on to Life's goal.

How bright would thy pathway be here, sinner,
    If like Enoch thou walkedst with God;
For the light of Heaven's day illumines the way,
    That the prophets and martyrs have trod.
There world-sorrows cease, there our spirits find peace,
There, while earthly lights pale, heavenly glories increase.

Hast thou done fell despite unto grace, sinner?
    Hast thou gloomy forebodings of wrath?
Still, still heavenly grace fully meets thy sad case,
    And with pardon now stands in thy path.
Now cleans'd from thy guilt, thou may'st go if thou wilt,
To the city which God for his people has built.

Has thy bark, without compass or chart, sinner,
    Sail'd forth on life's treacherous main?
Art thou now wildly toss'd? Is thy hope wholly lost?
    Dost thou look for a haven in vain?
In Christ there is rest for all spirits distress'd,
In Him now thou may'st of all good be possess'd.

P

Hast thou wounds which even time cannot heal, sinner?
　The Saviour for thee has a balm;
Does the wild winter storm all thy prospects deform?
　Jesus offers thee sunlight and calm.
On Jesus now lean, and 'mid life's troubled scene
Thy spirit shall bask in Heaven's daylight serene.

What joy there would be over thee, sinner,
　If thou wert renew'd and forgiven;
All the holy with thee would in sympathy be
　And encourage thee upward to heaven.
O then thou would'st see in hill, vale, and tree,
A glory before all unknown unto thee!

Bird, beast, verdant hill, leafy tree, sinner,
　And the flower springing fresh from the sod;
Yea, all nature would be as a ladder to thee,
　On which thou would'st rise to thy God.
In morn's orient gold, in night's glories unroll'd,
In all nature around thou thy God would'st behold.

Like a bird from the fowler escaped, sinner,
　Thou would'st carol in Heaven's summer glow,
And sweet would be toil, for thy Father's bright smile
　Would rest on thy life here below;
Thy spirit would sing, and mount on glad wing,
And drink in the fragrance of life's joyous spring.

Thou would'st sit 'neath Christ's shadow with joy, sinner,
　·And know at His bright ample feast
The sweet foretastes of heaven known by rebels forgiven;
　Yea, His fruit would be sweet to thy taste.
O what state is so fair as those of Heaven's heir?
What prospect with His can one moment compare?

How sweet to lie down every night, sinner,
    And to think, ere a new morning shines,
O'er my wandering soul the light-floods may roll
    Of that morning that never declines,
And Heaven's joys may be mine, and such splendour divine,
As all that of heaven I have dream'd would outshine.

How sweet to wake morn after morn, sinner,
    And to think that the Lord is thy God,
Thy Father and Stay, and the Guide of thy way,
    Who saves thee and bears all thy load.
Who thy life doth illume, and o'er the dark tomb
Makes Hope's beauteous garlands most brightly to bloom.

How sweet 'tis to think of that dawn, sinner,
    When all who in Christ fall asleep,
At the trumpet's shrill sound shall arise from the ground,
    The harvest of glory to reap ;
When, all ended their sighs, and made meet for the skies,
Living saints shall mount up to receive Life's fair prize.

O why wilt thou madly remain, sinner,
    Unmeet for yon home in the skies?
Why still sin embrace?   Why still take thy place
    Among those who the Saviour despise?
O ne'er canst thou know what of suff'ring and woe
Jesus bore, that Life's crown He on thee might bestow.

The summer will come to an end, sinner,
    And the harvest will quickly be past,
Doom may be deferr'd, and the rebel be spar'd,
    Doom comes to the rebel at last.
Though thou, in thy sky, dost no portent descry,
The dreadful tornado of wrath may be nigh.

Christ will send down His angels to reap, sinner;
　　With the wheat they to heaven will return;
With unquenchable fire, O judgment most dire!
　　The reapers the chaff then will burn.
O now, timely wise, seek a home in the skies;
Flee, flee from the worm and the death that ne'er dies.

Come to Jesus while thou hast the light, sinner,
　　Lest night fall, and no light on before
Thy vision should mark, and on sin's mountains dark
　　Thou stumble to rise up no more.
Draw nigh unto God by the sin-cleansing blood,
And the treasures of grace shall on thee be bestow'd.

Haste, haste to a merciful Lord, sinner,
　　Despise not the free grace of God;
To-day be thou saved, even now be thou lav'd
　　From thy sins in the fountain of blood.
O think what it cost ere the ruin'd and lost
Could be sav'd and could shine 'mong the bright heavenly host!

Didst thou come to the Saviour now, sinner,
　　What joy might'st thou bring to thy race!
By thee Heaven's great King would make wells to upspring
　　In many a desolate place.
What wastes dark and bare, by the Lord's Gospel-share,
Thou might'st turn into gardens most fruitful and fair.

There is glory and honour for thee, sinner,
　　And the Triune Jehovah says "Come,"
And on Canaan's bright coast the vast ransom'd host
　　And the angels all beckon thee home.
And the saints on earth cry, "Sinner, why wilt thou die
When God His salvation to you has brought nigh?"

Like a jasper most precious and clear, sinner,
   Is the city and home of the blest;
And you may go in and Life's glorious crown win,
   And partake of the heavenly rest.
How ineffably sweet with God's pilgrims to meet
In that home with all beauty and glory replete!

Again the preacher pauses, and much need,
After delivering such lengthy screed—
Much need to pause for breath.   Behold him now:
Absorb'd in earnest thought, he strokes his brow;
Ah, one would say he now has reached the end.
Yet 'tis not so.   His powers he soon doth bend
Towards something further, one more loving word
To win men to the Lamb, God's Son, his own dear Lord.

CONCLUSION.

Gaze on Christ's wounds, as I have done,
   Until you love Him;
See Him the wine-press tread alone
   Until you love Him;
O hear the bleeding God-man cry,
" Is't nought to you, ye that pass by,
That in your room and stead I die,
   'Neath God's fierce anger?"

O Christ!   Thine embassy of love
   My soul transporteth;
Thy finish'd work doth quite remove
   The curse from off us;
Whereas we, groaning 'neath sin's weight,
Could make no hairbreadth towards Heaven's gate,
Thy finish'd work doth bring us straight
   To God and glory!

O greatest sight of time and worlds !
    Sure angels wonder'd,
And knowledge gain'd of God, when He
    Who might have thunder'd
On earth in wrath, a man became,
The meekest that bore human name,
Yea, died by man on cross of shame,
    For man's salvation.

O greatest sight of time and worlds !
    Interposition
Of God on guilty man's behalf,
    That strikes my vision !
What meaneth this ?   Could nought suffice
For worms but God a sacrifice ?
Could nought but He become the price
    Of my redemption ?

No ! only great Immanuel's life
    And death-transaction
Could be to God's dread holy law
    A satisfaction
Abundant, so I might go free ;
Yea, thus and only thus to me
God's glorious righteousness could be
    By God imputed.

O fathomless, sweet mystery !
    What declaration
Of God is this which I do see ?
    Imagination

Spoke of a hard taskmaster-God;
But man so loving never trod
This earth as He; lo! even His blood
    He gives to save us.

Behold, behold the dying God
    Until you love Him!
His face and form are smear'd with blood,
    Men, devils, prove Him;
Men, devils, rage; earth's hope seems gone,
While He the wine-press treads alone.
Yet this is victory; Hell's o'erthrown
    By His submission.

Sinner! see Nature veils her face
    While her Creator
Doth take the guilty sinner's place.
    More cause than Nature
Hast thou to veil thy face with woe:
Thy sin did bring thy God thus low;
Thy sin, too, and its fruits of woe,
    His cross has ended.

Gaze on Christ's wounds, and gaze again
    Until you love Him;
God as the Lamb for sinners slain
    Can make us love Him.
We thought of a taskmaster-God;
But man so loving never trod
The earth as He; lo! even His blood
    He gives to save us.

Thus the old man, in lofty style and brave,
Brings to a close his exhortations grave ;
Then, his right hand uplifting, he commends
His work to Him who spiritual fruitage sends ;
Invokes God's blessing on the people round,
Prays that their names may every one be found
In the great Book of Life ; that for the sake
Of Him who did our sins and troubles take
Upon Himself they may, one day set free
From trial, know blest immortality.
Thus prays he, and breathes forth his deep amen,
Just when the old town clock is striking ten.
Chime after chime rings out deep, clear, and loud,
And motionless he stands amid the crowd,
Till sounds the last—Some Christian folks now press
Up to him, take his hand, and glad express
Themselves as edified with what they've heard ;
And two, at least, in their new-roused regard
For the dear veteran man, forthwith invite
Him to come home and spend with them the night.
Whereat the old preacher's eyes most grateful shine ;
Yet he most certainly must now decline
One of the invitations—howe'er loath
To decline a good, he can't accept them both.
Therefore he warmly thanks the one dear brother
Whose offer he declines ; and with the other
Goes to enjoy a hospitality
Most homely ; a communion blythe and free !
Adieu, old preacher ; my good friend, adieu !
God bless thy stout old heart so kind and true.

PART IV

Elegiac Poems.

ELEGY ON THE DEATH OF THE REV. THOMAS DAVIDSON.

Manibus date lilia plenis :
Purpureos spargam flores.　　*Virgil.*

ROLL on thy way,
O crystal Jed ; roll on, and sing
'Midst birch and hawthorn bourgeoning—
Round rocky scaur and woodland steep ;
　Roll on, thou limpid stream !
Thy murmurs cannot break his sleep,
　Nor steal into his dream !
　Roll thro' the glory and the gleam,
　'Neath stellar ray and lunar beam,
　　O ripple soft beside the shade,
　　Where oft the dreaming poet stray'd,
And woo'd high Fancy from her mystic throne—
　　O ripple gently, gently on !
Thy song is not as it has been of yore ;
　　A thought of grief is in thy tone ;
The Genii of thy caverns now deplore,
　　And fling on every breeze a hollow moan.
　　　　Nor Summer's light nor Autumn's gold,
　　　　In shadowy splendour o'er thee roll'd,

Thy light, thy glory will restore,
 Since he, the Muse's favourite son,
Who lov'd to croon the mountain lay,
Or drink the mystic streams of antique lore,
 Or dream bright dreams thro' the long summer day,
Or list thy waters lap thy pebbled shore,
Shall join his sounding lyre with thine no more !

  Let no sepulchral yew
 Hang her long tresses o'er his couch of rest ;
  Let no funereal shade
  Over him be made,
 Whose spirit now rejoices 'mong the blest ;
 Let the young spring's mouth
Upon his grassy mound be earliest prest ;
 Let beauty from the south
 His narrow house invest !
 Let lilies, virgin white,
And daisies of sweet modest dyes,
And delicate anemones,
And violets with tender eyes,
Bloom bountifully o'er the youthful poet's grave :
 Lilies to symbol forth his purity,
 Daisies to tell how meek his spirit was,
 And violets and anemones—alas !
Let these declare how soon his soul did pass
 Away from cold and dull mortality
 To join the good and brave !
Let Summer's most enduring garland wave
O'er him whom neither mortal love nor tears could save,
  O'er him who drew

All light and glory unto him,
　Till even this fair earth grew dim
Before his spirit's bright eternal hue !
　　Let the saintliest hymn,
　With which true love her ardours may declare,
　Warbled by some sweet spirit of the air,
　　　Rise softly, sweetly, holily,
　　　O'er him who lieth holily,
O'er him whose music flowed so rich and rare,
　　　That Love, with sweetest charity,
　　　Gently took him home to be
A singer in her temples bright and fair !

MRS. CRAIK, AUTHOR OF "JOHN HALIFAX, GENTLEMAN," 1888.

'Twas when the woods were deck'd in gold,
　And fields a faded garment wore ;
'Twas then her hand in death grew cold —
　Her hand to wield the pen no more !

Yes, she is gone, the woman brave,
　Who did so well instruct our youth
In life's strange mystery ; she who gave
　Us gems of beauty, gems of truth ;

She whose fine page, when nights were long,
　Did chain us round the ruddy fire ;
She whose true story and rich song
　Could never pall, could never tire.

Her pen now lies aside unus'd ;
　　Her work is done ; what's writ is writ ;
Ah, may it be the more perus'd
　　Now the last period's put to it !

Who runs may read it and may know
　　That it was done by woman true ;
One quick alike in joy and woe,
　　One who sun-glances round her threw ;

One who right into being's heart
　　Could look and see what things were there ;
One who still nobly did her part,
　　To combat darkness and despair ;

To bring in light and hope, and all
　　That bright inheritance of good
Which God makes to our portion fall
　　'Neath His protecting Fatherhood.

From what she to her readers penn'd,
　　This gifted soul we only knew ;
Yet oh, we felt she was a friend,
　　One of the truest of the true.

The kind pulsations of her heart
　　We felt ; yea, it was ours to know
How lib'rally she could impart
　　Of her large nature's overflow.

And still thro' life's wild maze to guide
　　Our feet ; our interests to promote —
For that like glorious sunlit tide
　　Roll'd on the treasures of her thought.

A woman on the side of God—
   A cultur'd, true, and shining soul ;
Her fulness she on us bestow'd,
   And therefore we her worth extol.

Still in our mental sight she stood,
   As only shining worth can stand,
Among that gifted sisterhood
   Who are an honour to our land.

It was her glory here to trace
   A hero after truth's high plan ;
To show that he, whate'er his place,
   Was still the brave, true gentleman.

It was her glory to assert,
   That whatsoe'er our difference here,
In place or state, the noble heart
   Is of the noble still the peer.

Yes, she deserves our praise ! her words
   Did act on us like sacred fire ;
Did strike our being's loftier chords,
   And lead us high and ever higher.

Her joy 'twas still to teach us love,
   Courage, endurance, loyalty ;
To stir us up to rise above
   All that may here against us be !

Still what of wisdom here she learn'd,
   What knowledge gain'd by effort brave,
Into " a cup of strength " she turn'd,
   A cup which she to others gave.

Unto the last 'twas her's to impart
　　The treasures of a noble mind ;
The deep experience of a heart
　　That knew the burden of mankind.

Like some rich tree, right on to age
　　She pleasant fruit around her cast ;
'Twas while we read her latest page
　　We heard that she from us had pass'd.

And mournful feelings on us press'd ;
　　Yet soon we to ourselves did say,
"God has His servant laid to rest
　　After the toilsome, weary day.

" Her work is now her legacy,
　　Her books will still instruct and cheer,
The richer and the happier we
　　Because she liv'd and labour'd here."

CHARLES WEBB, SHOEMAKER, JEDBURGH.

JUST when upon us op'd the flowery year ;
　　While yet the anemone did our woods adorn ;
　　Ere yet the blossom burst upon the thorn ;
Just then thou left us, our old friend so dear.

Thou modestest of Nature-loving men !
　　Then wert thou lost unto the banks of Jed,
　　And to the Dunion Moor.   Now I shall tread
The accustom'd paths, nor see thee there again.

Of the lov'd scenes thou hadst e'en grown a part ;
   But thou 'mang these, O friend, no more wilt walk ;
   No more there blend with me in peaceful talk,
In grateful interchange of mind and heart.

No more ! these words, alas ! sound sad and strange ;
   Yet who has here a permanent abode ?
   We seek a city bright whose builder's God ;
There only are we safe from painful change.

And to that city thou hast sought thy way,
   And now I'd say a word in praise of thee
   Who verily hadst no common charm for me,
Who for thyself hadst simply nought to say.

Yes, thou dost merit praise ; thou who so long
   Didst keep the even tenor of thy way,
   Facing the humble duties of each day
With tranquil soul, with faith devout and strong.

I testify that thou wert here, O friend,
   A son of toil of noblest ancient type,
   Whose thoughts amid laborious calm grew ripe,
Whose mind still upward did serenely tend.

A personality was thine on which
   I well may ponder with a soul elate ;
   Far greater wert thou here than many great ;
And richer far, though poor, than many rich.

I joyful think of thee even as of one
   Who wert distinguished and unique in much ;
   One who with Nature was in happiest touch,
Who lov'd all pleasant things that love the sun.

And oft will I recall those seasons bright
    When I with thee did walk our rural ways,
    And gave to thee the unstinted meed of praise
While our grand Scottish lays thou didst recite.

'Mong the old scenes I'll pause and pause again,
    And say, 'Twas here he nobly did repeat
    Graham's "Sabbath"—here that "Hymn" sublimely
        sweet
Which Thomson sang—here this or that high strain!

Even on such wise I'll oft remember thee,
    And see thy face as in the vanish'd time,
    And hear thy tones pathetic, grave, sublime,
And live again the hours we us'd to see.

ON VISITING THE GRAVE OF THOMAS AIRD, ST. MICHAEL'S CEMETERY, DUMFRIES.

AND lies he here, the gifted man who sang
    That strange, magnificent song, the "Devil's Dream;"
    The man whose genius, like seraphic beam,
Smote on me early; he whose music rang

Early like tocsin through my deepest soul,
    Awakening many a heavy slumbering power,
    And urging me to use the day and hour,
And push ahead unto some worthy goal?

Yes, here he's laid—here do his ashes lie—
    With awe I mark the final resting-place
    Of him whose soul o'erwelled with light and grace;
Whose eye was in high sense the poet's eye;

Who saw into this life of mystery—
  Mark'd its dark shadows and its gleaming lights,
  Its solemn depths and its sun-gilded heights,
Its features, too, of mirth and pleasantry;

Who look'd on Nature as a glorious friend—
  A friend withal of sweetest homely grace;
  Who dwelt on the expressions of her face,
And on her charm and interest without end.

Verily, of my lov'd Aird I will assert
  That he was here a grand and kingly soul;
  That with high aims his song he did outroll,
And well fulfill'd a sacred singer's part.

Yea, I will speak for those admiring few
  Who love him well; and in their name will say,
  He was a son of the celestial day,
Whose genius many a sterling picture drew;

Whose verse, so mark'd by bright heroic gleams,
  So rich with life's fine art and spirit brave,
  And Nature's wealth, is fitted well to save
Us from a pseudo-art's vain puerile dreams;

Is fitted well within us to upbuild
  Ideals true, and foster manly worth;
  And make this dwelling-place of ours, God's earth,
For us more rich, more with high beauty filled.

———

ON AN OLD FRIEND AND EXEMPLAR.

LONG years have gone since I beheld thee last;
   Long years hast thou with all on earth been done;
   Yea, since thy going many a cherish'd one
Has o'er the strange mysterious boundary pass'd.

Yet in my memory thee still fresh I find—
   Fresh still before me shines thy speaking face:
   I mark thy features, still I on them trace
The attrition of the earnest working mind.

I see thee as I wont so long ago
   To see thee yonder in the well-known school:
   Again, O master, learn'd and beautiful,
Thou mak'st my soul with love of knowledge glow.

After long years 'tis fresh in me to-day
   How thou didst make my novice thought aspire
   And mount aloft, even as on wings of fire,
By this thing and that other thou didst say.

Nought that was for our good didst thou omit;
   Yea, was there aught of art and poetry
   That had administer'd a joy to thee,
That gav'st thou us even as thou sawest fit.

Ah, thou wert dear to us, thy rattling boys;
   Yet not till thou didst for another scene
   Take thy departure did we feel, I ween,
What lay beneath thy well-known look and voice.

We heard of thee that thou wert toiling on,
   Laying up store of intellectual wealth ;
   We never thought of thy sore-failing health,
Of thy life-strength fast going and nigh gone !

At length unto our town thou didst return,
   A man of learning vast, as we could see ;
   A man with thoughts of cultur'd brilliancy,
But with a bodily frame fatigu'd and worn.

O that sad day thou said'st thy last good-bye!
   I little thought thou would'st be laid away
   From " the warm precincts of the cheerful day "
So soon, so soon ! thy hopes were yet so high.

Yet, after all, 'twas Heaven that did to thee
   Appoint life's term—and wise are all Heaven's ways ;
   And life's not measurable by its days,
But by its purpose and nobility.

A gentleman wert thou—yes, every inch—
   A man right loyal, true, considerate,
   Who would no jot of truth or duty bate,
Who from the noblest standards would not flinch ;

A man who'd stand up strong for what was good,
   Even though the whole wide world might 'gainst him
      speak;
   A man who would not popular favour seek,
Who look'd to God, not to the multitude ;

A man of clearest head, of warmest heart—
   One, too, who might in letter'd fields have thriven—
   One who would anywhere have wrought for Heaven,
And acted out a bright heroic part ;

A man, indeed, in heavenly love baptiz'd ;
For to the seeing soul 'twas evident
That thou into a needy world wert sent
To impart among us the remedial Christ.

Yes, I will praise thee !—who doth merit praise
More than that man so kind, so lovable—
That man more beautiful than I can tell—
The friend and teacher of my early days ?

Ay, who ? I ask ; and fain would I hand on
Something of thee, thou noble Christian soul—
Something which, while the days and seasons roll,
Might tell how lovely was my friend long gone.

Fain would I show what courage thou hadst here ;
What gentle, yet invincible true love ;
How thou right onward to the end didst move,
Surrounded by a gracious atmosphere.

Thy faith, thy beauty, I would fain reveal
In noblest verse, and say, This, this is he
Who show'd a high example unto me,
Who wrought and pray'd for my eternal weal :

My master dear whose record is on high,
Whose fame, methinks, even now is noised abroad
Far in the Kingdom and the City of God,
Whose praises there, I trow, shall never die.

ON MY BOY'S DEATH.

WE heard thee blow thy bugle-horn,
  Teaching thy sister melody,
Richard! upon the very morn
  Of the sad day when thou didst die.
The night before thou would'st not rest,
  Save with thy hand enclasp'd in mine:
Such kindness glow'd within thy breast,
  Such love, such loyalty divine,
Dear child, thou to thy father borest
When grief with him was at the sorest;
Thus didst thou rest in slumber deep
  So silently, so silently,
We fear'd thee fallen on death's long sleep,
  And our hearts beat fitfully.
So strangely pale and still
  Lay thou upon thy bed,
That our hearts did quivering thrill
  With fears that thou wert dead.
But when the morning forth did shine,
A stir of life again was thine—
  Thou wert reviving!
Anon—even as I said—we heard thee blowing
Thy little bugle, thus most plainly showing
  The glorious joy thou felt among the living.

O, wingèd joy! full soon did press
On thee a solemn weariness;

Rightly did we opine
That thou wert nigh thy final bliss,
And that the utter sacredness
Of death would soon be thine.
'Twas afternoon in a fair June-earth
When thine eyes were waxing dim,
And the forests gay had stayed their mirth
To chant thy parting hymn.
Now stood we round our dying boy
In tears and breathless awe,
And a sudden, strange, o'ermantling joy
Soon in his face we saw:
A smile of bright seraphic grace
Sudden diffus'd upon his face—
Sudden diffus'd and sudden pass'd—
And we had seen our darling's last.
Oh, to us mortals had been given
A glimpse, a precious glimpse of heaven!
But what of heaven we could not see,
Of that let us think reverently.

Sweet pansies pull'd I from thy mother's grave,
And laid them on thy death-chill'd breast,
And to thy hand a yellow rose I gave—
A Howden rose; thus for the cold grave drest,
Even like some seraph-sleeper thou didst rest
Within thy coffin; or, I'd better say,
Thus did thy tenement of clay rest there—
For, O, the living Richard was elsewhere!—
He upon ardent wing had shot afar
Beyond or earth, or sun, or moon, or star,

And now was in the uncreated day
  With her who bore him, and with all the good
And brave who in Christ's name have fought their way
  Up to life's apex and beatitude.
O yes! to such high eminence thou wert rais'd,
  So high wert mounted o'er the starry spheres,
It was the mortal part on which I gaz'd,
  The immortal was with God—no need for tears!
No need for tears!—God's hand undid the door
  Of the poor cage, and let His lyrist fly
To amaranthine bowers, therein to pour
  Uninterrupted his rapt melody.

Yet, O my bird, my bonnie bird,
  That sang to me sae cheerily,
Since last thy tender song I heard
  I've trod the world fu' wearily.
O yes! thou wert a friendly stay
To me upon life's rugged way,
And less than human I would be
Were I not lonely, reft of thee!
My boy! my darling only boy!
  I miss the solace of thy face,
  And all thy fine, unconscious grace,
And thy young-hearted joy!
I miss thee breaking into rippling or explosive laughter
  Over each little humorous thing,
And hovering, hovering thereafter
  Upon joy's wing!
What though to-day, even as of yore,
Gay throstles in the forests pour

Their lyrics sweet?   What though the trees
Now hang with rich embroideries?
What though ilk bonnie wayside flower
Has a voice of hope for the cloudy hour?
Not all, not all this bright revealing
   Of Nature which I hear and see,
From a strange, aching, lonesome feeling
   Can wholly set me free.
I miss thee! something human and divine,
A tender something's gone out of this life of mine!

IN MEMORY OF ALEXANDRINA M——.

WHAT time my Highland sister died,
Alas! I was not by her side;
I only came in time to pay
The last sad office to her clay:
A tear o'er her lov'd dust to shed,
Then let it down among the dead.

'Twas on the slopes of Tobermory,
All in the summer's waning glory,
While holy deep tranquillity
Was far diffus'd o'er land and sea,
We laid our sister down to rest
With feelings not to be express'd.

Ah, yes, her faithful life was past,
And she was noble to the last!
Her simple story could I tell,
Would serve but this, to show how well
On earth she lov'd and was belov'd;
How lovely in her sphere she mov'd.

What though she might with loveliest grace
Have fill'd some high distinguished place,
Humbly, with her who gave her birth,
She chose to live her life on earth;
To be that lov'd one's earthly stay,
To smooth for her life's rugged way.

Loving, magnanimous, and true,
She did what here she found to do;
To conscience, God's vicegerent, still
Bending her wishes and her will;
Living her life with fix'd regard
To Him who is His saint's reward.

Yes, she as Christ's own handmaid here
Was found still faithful in her sphere;
Her sphere which did full well suffice
To test her powers of sacrifice;
To show what virtue she possess'd,
What truth was on her soul impress'd.

And while the days succeed the days,
Oft will we mention her with praise;
Oft find in her deep loyalty,
And all her silent victory,
Something which we, to failure prone,
With profit still may muse upon.

And on my soul she oft will rise,
As first she shone before mine eyes,
An apparition, young and bright,
Of power to put all clouds to flight;
To cheer, to inspire with healthful mirth,
To show that joy was still on earth.

Yes, she was then full rich in hope,
And, like the sprightly antelope,
Grace in her every movement show'd,
And joy on all her features glow'd ;
Old age, it seem'd, she ne'er could know—
Ah, it at length has prov'd even so.

Still young, still young, the lov'd has gone,
And O, thou mother sad and lone,
The cup which thou hast had to drink
Through the long years—of that I think !
O, that thou might'st be comforted,
That thou might'st lift thy weary head !

I see thee weeping in the night ;
Yet joy will come with morning light !
Fear not ! thou on the eternal shore
Wilt meet the lov'd, to part no more ;
Yes, thou wilt find thy daughter there,
With Heaven's own glory bright and fair.

IN MEMORY OF A BELOVED SISTER.

DEAR Sister Maggie, might I now
    For thee awake the lyric string ;
Some song, with brother love aglow,
    Might I unto thy memory sing !

And surely the dear thought of times
    Long gone, of youth and youthful glee,
Might well awake some artless rhymes,
    Might well call forth a song to thee.

O, dear old times, when thou, a girl,
    Dost 'mong the band of sisters shine,
A bright surpassing flower, a pearl,
    A human margarita fine :

When thou didst make the old farmhouse ring
    Full many a day, full many a night ;
For like a skylark thou could'st sing,
    And still in soaring hadst delight.

But came the end of girlhood gay,
    A wife belov'd thou didst become ;
And ere long time had passed away,
    Fair household plants did round thee bloom :

Fair household plants, a numerous band,
    Soon, sister dear, did round thee bloom ;
But ah, the end was near at hand,
    And thou wert waning to the tomb.

Sudden the summons came—ah me !
    When thou wert call'd death's cup to drink ;
Thy husband and thy family
    Stood still, not knowing what to think.

And well they might ; for surely then
    At awful speed for them this scene
Was changing, and no more again
    The world would be as it had been.

Yes, changes sad were being wrought,
    Changes within the happy home
Beginning, which beyond all thought
    Might have an influence on some.

'Twas so; yet thanks to Him who is
　　The arbiter of each event,
Peculiar wisdom, guidance, grace,
　　Were with the heavy trial sent.

Through the thick darkness many a ray
　　Of precious heavenly solace shone,
And mourners wept, yet learn'd to say,
　　Let God's most holy will be done!

Let God's most holy will be done!
　　Amen! say we: it must be best;
Mistake with Him there can be none,
　　So in His pleasure let us rest.

Still let us bravely rest us there,
　　And let us muse with thankful mind
On what of noble, good, and fair,
　　'Twas ours in the belov'd to find.

Ah yes, of thee, dear sister, whom
　　I speak of now, I well may say,
Thy virtues were God's flowers, whose bloom
　　And fragrance cannot pass away.

Whene'er I think of thee, I see
　　One of the gentlest who e'er trod
The path of true nobility,
　　The way that leads through Christ to God.

With all on earth thou wert at peace,
　　Thy mission plainly was to bless;
Nor from welldoing didst thou cease,
　　And good without obtrusiveness.

A LAST TRIBUTE.

INTRODUCTORY.

GREAT poets by necessity more than choice
　　Man's deeply-chequer'd story still rehearse;
And in so doing give articulate voice
　　To this mysterious, passionate universe;
Articulate voice unto the yearning
　　Hope, Joy, Despair, and Woe
With which humanity's heart is burning;
　　And not obscurely show
Eternal Justice, the Unsleeping,
O'er mundane things His vigil keeping;
Nor mitigating ought of His high claims
In deference to titles, grandeurs, or great names.

Alack, I must come short, far short of this,
　　　In these memorials of thee:
　　　Enough it is to me
To image forth thine angel loveliness,
　　　As thro' the dusk of years
　　　It still to me appears;
Enough to represent thee walking here,
　　Thine inner eye fix'd on the eternal sun,
Thy soul fill'd full of blessed daylight clear,
　　Thy heart all love—so own'd by every one
Who read thee right.　Enough in mode direct
To speak of one who here was of no sect,
But who belong'd to God and to the race;
One who for every good could find a place,
And who commended God by her May-morning face!

Now standing by thy tomb I own, I own
That thou by wisdom strong within did'st rise
To virtues, dignities, nobilities
By me, until I knew thee, all unknown,
Or unattainable deem'd. I own that thou
Did'st practically show us how
We may achieve the good, the true, the fair,
And the blest will of Godhead do and bear
In every circumstance of passing life.
Rest, sweetly rest, then, from the weary strife
Of good and evil, in the which can be
For us no pausing, no neutrality,
As long as we are journeyers 'neath the sun.
O take thy rest! thy work so nobly done
Has earn'd it well if e'er 'twas earnèd well;
Yea, Christ Himself methinks shall one day tell
How true thou wert, how gentle and how loving!
Rest on! things here assuredly are moving
To wondrous pre-determin'd consummations;
And yet thou shalt mount up 'mid jubilations
Of angels and all blest intelligences
To receive those gifts and holy recompenses
Which Christ shall give to faith—the fulness bright
Of Him who is thy Lord, thy King, thy Life, thy Light.

PART I.

Oh, I remember how, on Minchmuir's brow,
The hoar frost lay like ashes, while we bore thee
To thy last resting-place. Long years since then
Have pass'd, and much with me has come and gone;
But all things have conspir'd to make me feel
More deeply that high worth that shone in thee.

Now, looking back, it seems as if to me
An angel-presence had been lent awhile
By some bright world, where clear ingenuous truth
Pervades all being, and where love is law.
Oh, now from realms of thought thou look'st on me;
Thine eyes with love aglow, the seal of God
Upon thy forehead, and thy raven hair
Inwrought with blue forget-me-nots of heaven.

Forget thee? No! Oh, in this whirlwind life
Thou wert a thought of peace, an anchorage
For the poor heart. In a Sahara parch'd,
'Mid a fierce blinding sun, thou wert a screen,
Leafy and beautiful—a tree which gave
At once a grateful shade, and flowers, and fruit;
A fountain too—a fountain of rare joy:
But metaphors are weak to set thee forth.
'Tis rare that in our passage through the world
We meet with natures of such noble stamp,
So massive, so harmonious, so gay,
So generous as thine. Devoid of guile,
With open heart, with perfect dignity,
Thou still did'st bear thyself among thy race.
Thou wert a part of all with whom thou met—
A human being with attributes, feelings, thoughts,
Virtues and faults all beautifully human.

Yes, more than any I have ever known,
Religion made thee live religiously,
And as a daughter of the human race.
No transcendental life on earth thou sought'st,
No fact-translation of some bright ideal

Of theosophic dreamer.   Here content
Wert thou with truth in common forms and ways,
In the fulfilment of all common duty,
And ordinary offices of love.
A heroine of duty, thou didst lay
Thy womanhood alongside of thy work,
And do it with a whole-heart honesty.
Right faithfully thou did'st it ; yea, with method
From day to day; bringing it all to show
An exquisite symmetry; ordering all according
To the fair pattern of thy graceful mind.
Thy life was clear, and straight, and bold, and strong ;
Something inspir'd by God ; a refutation
Of error ; yea, a blessed declaration
Of what was true ; and more than any words,
It show'd how poor a thing is Mammon's creed.

Speak well I might of thy fair massive form,
The index bright of thy fair massive soul ;
I might make mention of thy pillar'd brow,
Round which thy raven locks in curls assembled ;
And of thy speaking eyes, large, blue, and deep
As crystal wells ; yea, of thy noble features
I in detail might speak ; yet, after all,
I would be forc'd to own it was the soul
That made the external form so passing fair.
Than thou, whose gaze was turnèd all through life
To the Eternal Sun, there was not here
A loftier, benedictory human presence,
Nor one more gay.   With brighter woman-angel
Never did shepherd walk the heather hills !
Souls of thy lofty stamp are God's high work,

And still as such the fairest ornament,
The strength, the solace of humanity.
Such souls are given to be our ministers
In times of sorrow, and to gird our loins,
And send us forth to every noble work.
Such are the Almighty's aristocracy,
And such have blest dominion while they serve.

Oh, still remembrance turns to those hill-scenes
Where first I saw thee—scenes from which afar
I've wander'd long, yet which in memory hang
Undimm'd, untarnish'd by the dust of years—
Scenes where I liv'd as free as bounding roe,
Where riding in the rattling teeth o' the storm
I croon'd my song—scenes, above all, where stands
The house familiar, in whose windows gleam'd
At shut of day fair hospitable lights
Lit by thy hands to lure thy wanderer home!
Can I forget thee in the old hill-places?
Ah, no! within the chamber of my mind
The most admirèd is that likeness of thee
Which shows thee in thy matron beauty there
Doing the rites of hospitality.
How bright the scene when thou thy table spread!
Speech then was music; yea, rough prose gave forth
The aroma of the poetry of love.
Then was it good to hear thee range at large, ʼ
In clear, well-chosen speech, o'er many things,
Eliciting from all that thou did'st touch
Something that stirr'd our being's finer chords,
And woke us to a higher, nobler life.
Oh, they who could receive the beautiful—

R

They with affinity to God, the fount
Of truth and loveliness; such souls could prize
Thy company; such hail'd thee as a star
Lighting them on to splendid destinies.
Yea, the world-sear'd, beholding thee, were brought
To the acknowledgment that Eden hath not
All vanish'd from us; that the earth has still
Souls brimming o'er with the odorous morning freshness
Of the primal world; frankincense souls that make
An Eden of so much of this hard world
As comes within the circle of their power.

I said that in the chamber of my mind
The most admirèd is that portrait of thee
That shows thee in the old home a matron fair
Doing the rites of hospitality.
Yet, oh, I have another portrait of thee
In the same chamber, which for me possesses
A powerful, an unutterable pathos,
Mix'd with a high and holy militant faith.
'Tis that which shows thee after thou, through tears,
Had'st look'd thy last upon the dear hill-place,
And fairly enter'd upon that which prov'd
The finishing act of the drama of thy life.
And, oh, how powerfully it brings up all
Thou wert in these last years! Oh, fair, and brave,
And pilgrim-like wert thou upon life's road.
Obstructions did not damp thine ardour strong;
For God was mighty in the world for thee.
That mystery of redeeming love which brooded
Four thousand years o'er poor humanity,
Then openly, in servant-form, appear'd

Among us doing good ; that mystery
Of glory and of love, the Man of Sorrows,
Inspir'd thee, strengthen'd thee, made thee victorious
O'er all thy foes ; yea, He, the Light of lights,
From out thy darkness did ordain thee light :
Himself burst in upon thy prison-house,
Making therein wider and wider rents,
Till thou wert swallow'd up in victory ;
Till nothing but the Godhead was around thee,
Above, beneath thee !—

Oh, 'tis a grief too big for human heart
When suddenly, and in our sorest need,
We are bereft of presence like to thine ;
Of noble spirit who with us has shared
Life's various fortune, who chief joy has found
Amid our joy, who 'mid adversity
Has walk'd beside us, reinforcing us,
Bidding us hope for better days to come ;
Then are we apt to challenge death and woe
To do aught more.   Seems then the lamp of life
Put out for aye.   Soon haggard, pale despair
Over life's ruin broods, and the soul's calm
Becomes more terrible than her tumults wild.
'Tis strange if, after such a blow, the world
Be ever as before ; if memory be
Ever again more than a chamber grey,
With dead or wither'd leaves and flowers bestrown.

Though well I knew on that December day,
When Death his signet press'd upon thy brow,
That 'twas thy lovely mortal part that died,

And not thy glorious immortal part ;
Yet, oh, I felt down in my heart of hearts
That death of thine was as a mighty millstone
Flung crashing through my life, breaking it into
Infinitesimal fragments which I ne'er,
By any art, could piece again together
Into an unity.   And when I stood
Beside thy grave, as yet unfill'd, and bent
Down thereunto, I felt as if the worlds
Look'd on in solemn pause ; and when I heard
The clods sound hollow on thy coffin'd clay,
Then night, grim-spectral, terrible, came down
Upon my soul.   In its fifth and last great act
Seem'd the world's tragedy ; and I, frenzied, cried
To God to end it with the crack of doom.

Too painful 'tis to speak of days that follow'd
Thy burial-day—days when the bread I ate
Was steep'd in tears—days when my life was bow'd
Down to the grave—days when I walk'd amid
Sepulchres, spectres, images of sorrow—
Days when I, whether waking or asleep,
Ransacked the universe for the beloved,
And could not find her, for she was translated
To glorious realms afar !   Too painful 'tis
To tell how, finding my tumultuous grief
All unavailing, I engirt my soul
With the girdle of despair.   Enough ! such griefs
Fall to the portion of humanity.
Oh, ever it is our highest good to find
God and our work—what finds the wisest more ?

Farewell! Since in this strange and tragic scene
Time and oblivion so oft efface
From living hearts the image of the lost;
Since 'tis the lot, even of the good and fair,
To be remember'd long but by the few;
'Twere bold in me to say—howe'er thou wert
Distinguishable in thy day by all
That marks the noble out from common souls—
That thou wilt be by many remember'd long:
Yet, oh, there are at least two human hearts—
The one thy mother's and the other mine—
Who must retain thee while with life they beat.
Within these hearts thou still must be enshrin'd.
These hearts must sorrow yet for many a day
Over the period, early and abrupt,
Which death did put unto thy life, so fair,
So rich in hope. Oh, when thou wert with us
There was a life of glory in our life,
And when thou went that life's life went with thee!

Yet in our very sorrow there is mixed
A sacred joy! For He who went through death,
Destroying him who had the power of death,
He made thee conqueror. The falsely great,
And such as see no home in heaven, oft faint
Before the awful mystery of the Unseen;
Yea, oft cry out what time the fatal shears
Are at life's thread. But thou whom the grim spectre
Of fear ne'er terrified; thou to whom the Lord
Was an invisible friend still at thy side,
Did'st see a home in God's eternity;

And in God's peace pass'd o'er life's shadowy bourne
To the better land.   The Conqueror Christ,
He made thee conqueror.
Who made thee conqueror will raise thee up.
I will believe the captives of the grave
Shall be set free what time the blessed Christ,
The Resurrection-Angel, gives the word.
I will believe that thou shalt in thy lot,
At the end of the days, stand up in radiant form,
Like that humanity thy God now wears ;
That thou shalt then be crowned by the piercèd hand
Of the Man of Sorrows, whose bright image shone
Brightly in thee in thy humiliation ;
That in accomplished glory thou wilt then,
With lyric grace, move 'mong the cohorts bright
Of God's redeemed ; saluting thine old friends,
Hymning God's praise in fathomless sweet song.
Oh, amplest recompense of suffering virtue,
Accomplish'd coronation of thy hopes,
Full compensation of subserving love
And beautiful self-abnegations here ;
Bright consummation of a brave, true life—
A life of faith in Him who came to save !

PART II.

What pious soul has not enraptur'd hung
Over that scene so unutterably fair—
The wearied Jacob pillow'd on a stone;
The outward man sunk down in slumber deep,
But the inward man awake and all attent
To the most glorious vision—to wit, a ladder
Rear'd up on the earth, and reaching unto heaven;
A ladder on which ascending and descending
Are angels bright; and over which the Lord
Stands giving blessing! Well might Jacob call
The place the House of God, the Gate of Heaven.
Well might he name it Bethel, which was Luz.
And what a scene of glory, too, was that
Whereof 'tis said that as the patriarch journey'd
God's angels met him, and, he seeing, said,
" This is God's Host;" and then he gave the place
The name of Mahanaim! And, in fine,
What blessed consummation was attained
In that great Peniel-scene—that scene wherein
We see the patriarch wrestling with a man
Until the daybreak; bating not a jot
In the straining conflict; reinforc'd, outcrying,
" I will not let.Thee go till Thou hast blest me;"
Receiving all, yea, more than all he sought
In the new glorious name of Israel !

Even of such sort the patriarch's life of faith.
And what though we may think that such high life
Was but peculiar to the saints, while yet
Humanity had not journey'd far in time

From Eden blessedness; still true it is
That the Angel of the Lord encamps about
All those that fear him; true it is that Heaven
Still grants blest interviews to faithful souls;
That Bethels, Mahanaims, Peniels
Still wait on those who struggle thro' the dark
Into God's light. Ah! well thou knewest this,
Dear saint, of whom I write. For thee this world
Was God's, a place of hope, a vantage ground,
From which to mount to higher, nobler scenes;
A chamber in God's Universal House;
High in whose upper chamber, Father, Son,
And all the bright triumphant ones do dwell.

———

THESE to hand on thy passing loveliness!
These glean'd from the wild plaintive songs I sang
After I saw thine eyelids close in death.
And who that has received such legacy—
Such spiritual legacy as I have done
From friend departed, but must in his mode
Transmit it on to others, and to others?
Charge him with egotism as thou wilt,
Thus he oft does the highest of behests;
Thus, too, is he indeed one of those hearts
Down which as down an avenue doth flow
The precious light. He addeth light to light;
He brings accessions to the spiritual wealth,
The best possession of humanity.

———

OFT the thought will in me rise—
" When in death did close thine eyes,
    Did death quite of thee bereave us ? "
And my heart still answers thus :
" What true grace thou left with us,
    That can never, never leave us."

And well answers thus my heart,
For though tomb'd thy mortal part,
    And thy soul gone through death's portal,
Yet that loveliness of thine
In my heart of hearts doth shine,
    Glistening all in tears immortal.

And since true hearts ever are
Channels for all beauty rare,
    Hearts to hearts it onward sending,
Thy rare beauty, vanish'd one,
Shall from hearts to hearts pass on
    As a blessed power unending.

———

I PLUCK'D a flower by Teviot's stream,
    A sweet forget-me-not;
And up from my being's deepest depths
    A thousand thoughts it brought.

A thousand thoughts ?—yes, a thousand thoughts,
    And a thousand feelings, too ;
O thou whose heart was unmingled love,
    Adieu ! again adieu !

WHEN I've thought of thy form lowly lying,
  Then how have my sorrows o'erflow'd;
Yet how sweet 'tis to think that thy dying
  Was but thy home-going to God!
O joy, now thy life's brave endeavour
  With Heaven's radiant guerdon is crowned;
And thy rapture flows on like a river,
  For thy good—thy chief good—thou hast found.

Thou didst pass through these regions terrestrial
  With the seal of thy God on thy brow;
To the country and city celestial
  A pilgrim, O fair one! wert thou.
With a dignity, never found wanting,
  Thou thyself in this world didst demean;
Thou wert tilling, and sowing, and planting,
  And otherwise blessing this scene.

Thou wert here for a strength and a solace
  To humanity's poor bleeding heart;
Alike in the hut and the palace
  Thou could'st do thine all-beautiful part.
Still thy presence was like some bright morning
  Which a spell over all things doth bring;
To the last thou had'st all the adorning
  And the bliss of a forest in spring.

Life's poetry, life's sacred essence
  Wert thou unto me—yea, my faith;
I liv'd in thy beautiful presence;
  I died, O I died in thy death.

As in dreams now I see mortals striving
　　In ambition's hot fever and strife ;
I'm no more in the ranks of the living,
　　I pass as a phantom thro' life.

———

Oh, when clos'd thine eyes in death,
Oh, when pal'd thy beauty's wreath,
　. Of that moment I may say
That chill gusts of death and change
Fiercely blew through Nature's range,
　　And the world grew cold and grey.

And when on thy coffin-lid
Clods resounded harsh and dread,
　　Then each sound did strike a blow
On my soul like hope's deep knell,
And I bade to joy farewell,
　　And surrender'd all to woe.

———

Oh, thou who our footsteps attended,
　　Like an angel of love and of light ;
Oh, so young, and so brave, and so splendid,
　　Art thou gone? art thou hid from onr sight?
Ah, yes ! but 'twas Heaven that out-meted
　　Thy life, and though few were thy days,
Thy work it was nobly completed,
　　And thy name now we mention with praise.

Thy life, like a poor broken column
　Seems to some; yet 'twas round and complete;
And what though thy death was so solemn,
　'Twas ineffably glorious and sweet.
Befitting thy brief, bright existence,
　Thy last words were glorious and few;
Like a traveller fading in distance,
　Thou didst wave unto us thine adieu.

Adieu! for a while it was given thee
　To sweeten humanity's cup,
And to raise to the high and the heavenly
　Poor sordid existences up.
Thou wert here ever noble and loving;
　Thou wert here strong, melodious, and free;
As of one to Heaven's chimes ever moving,
　We still did take knowledge of thee.

———

WHAT time 'twas given to me to meet with thee
　Thou took'st me to thy sunny upper room,
Through whose high lattice we the heavens could see,
　And all whose space was fill'd with spring perfume;
And there and then, while thou didst talk with me,
　I felt deep in my heart that I had come
Unto a dwelling which the muses high
Did e'en regard with glad complacency.

O they who met with thee were not in haste
　To fly thy sweet and goodly company;
A table thou didst rear upon the waste,
　Where we might eat and drink right pleasantly;

Yea, vines more sweet than Eshcol's we did taste,
   And waters of more pure vitality
Than those of Jacob's Well we drank what time
We at thy board did mingle thoughts sublime.

'Twas thine to fill with blessed fruitfulness
   Each spot thy Father gave thee here to till;
For thy philosophy still lay in this—
   Man! find thy work, and do it with a will!
'Twas thine to make our grief and cumber less,
   Our pleasure more. How nobly thou didst fill
Thy place on earth, ah me! we know so well,
And to thine honour O so much could tell!

Homely Rhymes, &c., from the Banks of the Jed. By AGNES STUART MABON. Preface by Rev. JAMES KING, M.A. Crown 8vo. Price 3/6.

"A genuine poetic spirit breathes through all the poems, and that the author has a heart alive to the sympathies and affection of friendship is to be seen in very many of her productions."—*Hawick Advertiser.*

Frae the Lyne Valley. Poems and Sketches by ROBERT SANDERSON, West Linton, Peeblesshire. Price 3/.

Lyrics and Poems of Nature and Life. By JANET K. MUIR, Kilmarnock. Fcap. 8vo, 3/6.

"Your lines do credit both to your head and to your fancy, and are not unworthy of one of the muse's devotees, who is sprung from the same county as Burns."—*The Hon. G. P. Bouverie, late M.P. for the Kilmarnock Burghs.*
"The effusion of a singularly sincere and pious spirit, without any ostentation or cant, and expressed in a sweet and natural flow of verse."—*Rev. George Gilfillan.*

A Mediæval Scribe, and other Poems. By H. W. H. Price 5/.

Quiet Waters: Essays on some Streams of Scotland. By H. W. H. Price 2/6.

Contains—The Clyde at Bothwell—The Yarrow—By the Sannox Burn—By the Allan—The River Kelvin—The Eden—The Logan Burn—The Douglas Water—The Cluden—The Fairlie Burn—By the Nith—By the Nethan—The North Esk—The White Cart.

Lichens from an Old Abbey: Being Historical Reminiscences of the Monastery of Paisley, its Abbots, and its Royal and other Benefactors. Fcap. 4to, 7/6; bevelled boards, gilt, 10/6.

"A handsomely got up book; . . . written in a thoroughly sympathetic spirit, and with full knowledge; . . . pleasant, readable, not the least of its merits being its historical accuracy as to dates and facts."—*Scotsman.*
"These pictures are touched with an exquisite skill and feeling, a certain antique stateliness. . . . It is an admirable book, and its appearance in every respect harmonises well with its merits."—*Daily Review.*

College Echoes. Sketches and Scenes of University Life at Edinburgh. Contains Useful Information for Students. By DAVID CUTHBERTSON. Price 1/.

The Scottish Patmos. A Standing Testimony to Patriotic Christian Devotion. By J. MOIR PORTEOUS, D.D. Price 1/.

The Churches in Asia. Extracts from the Home Letters of Rev. A. N. SOMERVILLE, D.D., from the Region of the Seven Churches. Price 2s.

Home Lessons on the Old Paths; or, Conversations on the Shorter Catechism. Given in an attractive conversational style, and illustrated by anecdotes and pictures. By M. T. S. Royal 16mo, cloth, 2/6.

Peeps at Rome for Young Eyes. Illustrated. By Rev. ANDREW G. FLEMING, Paisley. Price 1/.

"A more excellent book, the object of which was to be interesting, instructive, and religious, we have seldom seen. Should prove an excellent Sabbath School prize."
"A well-written and interesting description of some of the most interesting sites and historical buildings in the famous Italian city."—*Scotsman.*

J. AND R. PARLANE, PAISLEY.   HOULSTON AND SONS, LONDON.

The Prince and the Peasant. An Operetta for Juveniles.
By ALAN REID, F.E.I.S. Sol-fa, 3d; Staff Notation, 1/.

Round ye Clock: A Sangspiel for Schools and Classes.
By ALAN REID. The salient features and the more humorous episodes
in an ordinary day of school life have been enlisted to render this
Cantata suited for performance by the scholars. Sol-fa 3d; Staff 1/.

The School Holiday: A Cantata for Schools and Classes.
Words by AGNES C. DEY. Music by ALAN REID. "One of the
most effective pieces for School Children." Sol-fa, 2d; Staff, 1/.

Freendship's Circle. A Cantata: Illustrative of the
Innocent Social Pleasures of Scottish Homes. Words by ALEXANDER
LOGAN. Music by ALAN REID. Sol-fa, 3d. Staff Notation with
Accompaniments, 1/.

The Braes o' Gleniffer: A Popular Reading on ROBERT
TANNAHILL and his SONGS. By ALAN REID. With 26 Songs
arranged for Part-Singing. Staff or Sol-fa. Price 3d.

Prince Charlie and the '45. Popular Reading, with 22 of
the best Jacobite Songs arranged as Solos, and for Part-Singing.
By ALAN REID. Staff or Sol-fa, 3d.

Lady Carolina Nairne and her Songs. Popular Reading
with 24 Songs arranged as Solos and for Part-Singing. By ALAN
REID. Staff or Sol-fa, 3d.

The Babes in the Wood: A Cantata for Schools and
Classes. Words by JAMES YOUNG GEDDES. Music by JOHN KERR.
Sol-fa 3d; Staff 1/.

Betsie's Story. Founded on Fact. By Rev. DAVID
MACRAE. A Scotch Reading illustrated with Song. The Music
(Seven pieces, including Temperance Anthem) arranged for four
voices. Sol-fa. Price 1½d.

Blind Bartimeus. A Sacred Cantata, for Baritone Solo,
Chorus, and Orchestra. By WILLIAM HUME. Sol-fa, 4d; Staff
Notation, 1/.

"Whilst the music makes no very severe demand upon the powers of an ordinary
choir, it is sufficiently educative to lead the tastes of musical amateurs. It is
expressive and appropriate, and is singularly well fitted for the study of musical
associations."

The Romance of Missions. A Popular Reading, containing
a short Biographical history of Christian Missions from the first
century to the present. With 18 Musical Illustrations Arranged for
Part-Singing. Staff or Sol-fa, 3d.

Homes and Haunts of Robert Burns. A Popular Reading,
by Rev. R. LAWSON, Maybole, with 19 Musical Illustrations from
Burns's Songs, specially arranged for Part-Singing. Sol-fa or Staff
Notation, 3d.

"Cannot fail to be popular in any part of the world where Scotchmen are congre-
gated. The musical illustrations are effectively arranged."
"It may be doubted if the Story of Burns' Homes and Haunts has ever been better
told."—*Scotsman.*

J. AND R. PARLANE, PAISLEY. HOULSTON AND SONS, LONDON.

THE NATIONAL CHOIR:

STANDARD SONGS &c. FOR PART-SINGING,

ORIGINAL AND ARRANGED,

ADAPTED for CHOIRS, CLASSES, and the HOME CIRCLE.

Staff or Sol-fa. PUBLISHING IN PENNY NUMBERS MONTHLY.

YEARLY PARTS I., II., III., and IV., with Prefaces by Prof. J. STUART BLACKIE; also Notes to the Songs—Historical, Personal, and Critical. Price 1/ each.

The FOUR YEARLY PARTS in ONE VOL., with Notes to the Songs, and Preface by Prof. Blackie Price 5/

Nothing better could be selected as a gift book for friends at home or over the sea than this large and varied collection of our finest National Songs.

"The arrangements are ably written."
"Really a National Handbook of Part Music."
—*Press Notices.*

SCHOOL MUSIC FOR THE STANDARDS. Edited by ALAN REID.

Part I. for Infants and Pupils in Standards I. and II. Price 1½d.
Part II. for Pupils in Standards III. and IV. Price 2d.
Part III. for Pupils in Standards V. and VI. Contains an Introduction to the Staff Notation, with Seven Pieces to illustrate the various Keys. Price 2d.
Part IV. Songs for the Upper Standards and for Advanced Classes. Price 2d; cloth 3d.

The Edinburgh Song-School. Select Songs arranged in Two and Three-part Harmony. By J. SNEDDON, Mus. Bac. Parts I., II., III., IV., V. Sol-fa, Price 2d. each.

The School Choir: A Collection of Songs arranged for Part Singing, with Exercises graded for the Standards. By W. H. MURRAY, G.T.S.C. Nos. 1, 2, 3, 4, 5, 6, 7, 8. Price 1d. each.

Tonic Sol-fa Vocalist: A Selection of School Songs suitable for Infant, Junior, and Senior Classes. By ALEXANDER ADAMSON. Price 2d.

The Progressive School Song Book. Arranged for Infant, Junior, and Senior Classes. Edited by JOHN BOGUE. Nos. 1 and 2. Price 1d. each.

The Normal School Vocalist. Select Pieces arranged for Three Equal Voices. With Elementary Notes. By D. B. JOHNSTONE. Staff Notation, 3d.; Sol-fa, 1d.

Graded Exercises for Sol-fa Classes. Compiled and Arranged by J. TANNAHILL. Price 1d.

J. AND R. PARLANE, PAISLEY.   HOULSTON AND SONS, LONDON.

www.ingramcontent.com/pod-product-compliance
Lightning Source LLC
Chambersburg PA
CBHW020341030726
47496CB00007B/1965